## About the Author

Born and raised in France, Muriel Maufroy worked as a journalist for the BBC World Service for many years. Today, she is studying Persian at the School of Oriental and African Studies, and has published a book of Rumi's quotations called *Breathing Truth*. She lives in London.

## Praise for RUMI'S DAUGHTER

'An exquisite evocation of a young woman's spiritual awakening . . . A poetic gift of the imagination as translucent and refreshing as water from a mountain stream.'

Anne Baring, co-author, *The Myth of the Goddess*

'A beautiful little book that speaks to the soul. The world of Rumi and Shams is seen through the eyes of a girl, full of simple wonder, wisdom and the mysterious turning of the heart. This story resonates with the sacred child and mystic in each of us.'

Llewellyn Vaughan-Lee, author of
*Sufism, The Transformation of the Heart*

'A profound record of psychological and spiritual transformation . . . Too soon over it is an inspiring read; evocative and heart stopping.'

*Self and Society*

# RUMI'S DAUGHTER

## Muriel Maufroy

### RIDER
LONDON · SYDNEY · AUCKLAND · JOHANNESBURG

First published in 2004 by Rider, an imprint of Ebury Publishing.
This edition published by Rider in 2005.

Ebury Publishing is a Random House Group company

Copyright © Muriel Maufroy 2004

Muriel Maufroy has asserted her right to be identified as the author of this Work in accordance with the Copyright, Designs and Patents Act 1988.

Lines from *The Four Quartets* by T.S. Eliot reprinted by kind permission of Faber and Faber. Every effort has been made to contact all copyright holders.

The Random House Group Limited Reg. No. 954009

Addresses for companies within the Random House Group can be found at
www.randomhouse.co.uk

A CIP catalogue record for this book is available from the British Library

Penguin Random House is committed to a sustainable future for our business, our readers and our planet. This book is made from Forest Stewardship Council® certified paper.

Printed and bound in Great Britain by Clays Ltd, St Ives plc

ISBN 9781844135837

Copies are available at special rates for bulk orders. Contact the sales development team on 020 7840 8487 or visit www.booksforpromotions.co.uk for more information.

To buy books by your favourite authors and register for offers, visit
www.randomhouse.co.uk

*To my mother*
*and*
*to Jean Gibson,*
*whom I still hear asking:*
*'Are you writing?'*

'See this rose
— the one most saturated with
the water of life now blossoming
most fully —
it will of necessity wilt before all
the other brides of the garden.'

JALAL UD DIN RUMI

THE PATH WAS BECOMING STEEP. AROUND HER THE TREES were now scarce, replaced by thorny bushes that kept clinging to her kaftan. She dropped her bundle of dry wood. Perhaps she should have waited for Aishel when the path had divided. On an impulse she had continued on the narrower path and now she wondered: Would Aishel have gone the other way? Should she go back?

She had reached a ridge from where she could see the purple mass of the mountain range stretching away and, above it, a few white clouds drifting lazily. She stopped to listen for Aishel's footsteps. A bird, somewhere on her left, sent out a trill. All around insects were buzzing in the morning heat. But there was no cracking of broken branches, no ruffling of dead leaves to indicate that her sister was approaching.

Had it been unreasonable not to wait for Aishel? Only a few days earlier her mother had entreated her, half smiling, half serious: 'Now that you are seven, you are to be reasonable.' Kimya knew Evdokia was talking about what she called her 'absences', those moments when she simply lost track of time and space. Kimya didn't understand what happened to her in those moments, nor did she ever know when they would come. So how could Evdokia ask her to be 'reasonable'?

دوست

She sighed, then stretched, enjoying the coolness of the air on her face. After a while she sat down on a rock, glad to be alone. Then it happened again: a force, a power, nailing her in stillness. Around her everything was now more vivid. The bushes, the rocks, the clouds drifting away – all seemed to be alive, their contours sharper, while within herself the same force was pulsing through her veins, engulfing her in its tremendous silence. She shut her eyes, overcome by the intensity of the experience. A single, high-pitched tone was vibrating in her ears, then it vanished and she felt herself falling into a bright, soundless joy.

She heard, at first faint, then louder, a voice calling her name. She noticed the insects humming again and the leaves rustling in the breeze. The rocks, the bushes, the clouds, all of them had lost their sharpness. At that moment Aishel appeared at the bend of the path, a large bundle of wood on her head.

'Kimya! Why didn't you answer when I called?' Her eyes, the same dark eyes as Kimya's, were bright with anger. 'I know, I know,' she said, 'you didn't hear me. You don't know what happened. But you never know what happens!'

Kimya was going to say that yes, it was true, she never knew. All she knew was that now she felt sad, and yet also happy. Was that not 'reasonable'? But she kept her thoughts to herself.

'Don't be angry. It's not my fault ...'

'Then whose fault is it?'

Kimya didn't answer. She picked up her bundle and they started to walk in silence down the path, back to the village.

It was the year 1239.

EVDOKIA WAS STANDING ON THE ROOF TERRACE, COLLECTING the clothes she had hung out to dry earlier in the morning. She was a large woman, in her early thirties, her face tanned and furrowed from working in the open air. Three children she had, and lucky to have them. She could still remember those, too many, who hadn't survived: one, only a few weeks old, struck by a strange fever which at the time had swept through the village, and Bahram, her dear little boy who was just starting to walk, found dead in his bed one morning. She sighed. It was not good remembering all that. She shouldn't complain. Her three children were in good health and growing: Tahir now sixteen, Aishel twelve, and Kimya, her youngest, just turned seven, whom, she must admit, she worried about. Oh, she was a lovely child, but so different from her other two! Tahir and Aishel had fallen and cried, spilled their food, rolled in the dust and messed up their clothes: in short, they had behaved like children and they still did. But Kimya! She was like no other child. She hardly ever cried when she hurt herself. And from time to time she fell into those strange moments when life seemed to spill out of her. She would stand still as though listening to some faraway sound or voice, apparently unaware of her surroundings, and her friends complained that she was no fun to play with.

Not that Evdokia didn't love her daughter. Kimya was so sweet

دوست

and so pretty with her large, dark eyes, her pale complexion and a way of carrying herself that made the women of the village remark that, one day, she would be a beauty. But that was no reassurance to Evdokia. She remembered the day, only a few months ago, when she had found Kimya in tears, huddled in the hollow of a tree near the vegetable patch.

'What's the matter? Why are you crying?' Kimya had looked at her with such sorrow in her eyes that Evdokia, too, had felt like crying.

'I was somewhere where I was so happy ...' And for a second it seemed the child had been touched by a beam of light. 'Then it was all over,' Kimya had sobbed.

Evdokia had taken her in her arms, feeling strangely inadequate, and they had stayed there for a while, surrounded by the smell of the bark and the earth, wet from the first autumn rain.

Since that day Kimya had kept even more to herself, falling so often into those absences that in the end her friends refused to play with her. She didn't seem to mind, though. She just sat looking at them as if from far away. And there were also those questions she kept asking.

'Why am I alive? Where was I before I was born?'

Evdokia would shake her head. Where does that child find such questions? she wondered. How will Kimya grow up? What will become of her?

Kimya was not by nature sad. She was full of life, always ready to laugh, always ready to jump to her feet whenever asked to help. But even when she was happy, she was different from the other children. Like those times when she burst into songs so full of joy

دوست

that Evdokia listened, startled, with the curious feeling of having heard those songs before.

This child has a way of upsetting me. She sighed. But what could be done? Kimya was Kimya and that was that. How does she happen to be mine? Evdokia asked herself. Kimya didn't quite belong here. She seemed to have been transplanted from some foreign land. Her husband, too, was concerned. Kimya was his favourite, though Farokh wouldn't quite admit it. But every night, after the last meal of the day, when Kimya was struggling to keep her eyes open, the same ritual took place that said more about Farokh's feelings towards his younger daughter than any of his words. He would take her in his arms while she put hers round his neck, and as he carried her to bed she murmured, 'Baba, Baba, I love you.' When Farokh came back and sat down, he had a beatific smile on his face.

Sometimes Evdokia made fun of him. 'That child is bewitching you!'

'Perhaps she is a kind of a witch, after all,' Farokh remarked one night as they were lying in bed, once again discussing Kimya.

Evdokia froze. 'Don't say things like that! I'm worried enough about her.' And the memory of the traveller of some eight years ago came back to her.

It was winter and already dark. She was then heavy with child. The village was buried in snow, the wind howling. Nobody in his right mind would have ventured outside, or so they thought. The family was gathered around the fire for the evening meal when the dogs started to bark. Then they heard the ice cracking under someone's feet. Farokh took the oil lamp and went to the door. A

دوست

burst of cold wind whirled into the room.

'Who is it?' Farokh shouted over the wind.

'*Salam aleikum* – peace be with you.' The voice was muffled.

'*Aleikum salam*,' Farokh answered. 'This is not a night to be out, my friend. Come in.'

The man entered, shaking off the snow from his coat. Slowly he undid the strips holding his leather soles, then unwrapped a large felt coat. Under it he was wearing a goat jacket, its fur turned inside out. His hair was grey like his beard, his face heavily wrinkled, but he had the sharp, alert eyes of a young man.

The children made room for the stranger who sat near the fire with a sigh of relief, followed by a great yawn that showed a mouth full of holes.

'My name is Mahsoud,' he said, but he didn't mention where he was coming from, nor where he was going.

'Here, have some tea,' Evdokia pressed him, 'and some bread and olives.'

He ate for a while without a word, and he was still eating when his head fell over his chest, and he started to snore.

The next morning the stranger helped to set the wood in the hollow of the wall that served as fireplace. His movements were slow and precise, and soon the ember left from the previous night leaped into a bright, orange flame.

'There we are,' the man said with satisfaction.

There was tea and what was left over from the previous night. The man ate in silence, then he looked at Evdokia.

'This baby,' he said, nodding towards her belly, 'this baby is going to be a girl. Her name will be Kimya.' He paused, then, as an after-

دوست

thought, he said, 'A great future awaits her.'

Farokh and Evdokia looked at each other. They didn't know what to say. Everybody knows that travellers are unpredictable, but this was different. This one had broken an unspoken rule; he had somehow intruded. The man finished eating as if nothing had happened. Then he wiped his mouth with the back of his hand and stood up.

'I must get on,' he said. 'I am on my way to Damascus. Thank you for your hospitality.' He wrapped himself again in his felt coat, and then, turning towards Evdokia, he added, 'Remember, the child's name is Kimya.'

Evdokia shivered at the memory. It was a long time ago, but the face of the man still haunted her at times. Lying next to her, Farokh was still awake. 'What should we do?' she asked him.

Farokh turned his head towards her. 'What about the imam? Perhaps he will have an idea. After all, he's supposed to be wise, and he talks to Allah.'

Evdokia was not sure the imam ever talked to Allah, but he was a good man. Why not ask him, indeed?

So Farokh went to see the imam who said he would pray and added, 'You must trust in Him who knows all and everything.' But he offered no advice.

And now Kimya was in her eighth year. Winter was back and soon the paths disappeared under thick layers of snow. Every morning when Farokh opened the door, he had to shovel the snow aside so they could make their way out. After a few days the entry to the house was reduced to a narrow lane squeezed between two walls of ice. The children got red cheeks and slid on the slopes, laughing at their breath turning into white clouds as they talked. Kimya, too, laughed and slid, but she also stood for long moments, looking at the mountains, blue and purple in the distance, and turning pink and crimson at sunset. Then it started.

Aishel once came back alone from a walk with Kimya. She was upset and angry.

'I was following her down the north valley where the vines are planted,' she said. 'She was running in front of me and then I couldn't see her any more. I looked around, I called her, but she was nowhere.'

'You mean, you left her behind!'

'I … I looked. I called her.' Aishel was close to tears.

'Where was it exactly?' Farokh asked.

'Near the two big rocks, you know, close to the vines. I looked around them, even through the gap in between. I called and called.' Now Aishel was crying. 'But she was nowhere.'

Evdokia took her in her arms. 'Don't worry.' She was stroking her hair. 'It's not your fault; she will be back. You know your sister has her own ways.'

And indeed, Kimya had come back several hours later as if nothing had happened.

'Didn't you hear me when I called your name?' Aishel was indignant.

Kimya looked at her; she didn't seem to understand. 'I sat on a rock for a while, then I don't know; I don't remember.'

'Leave her alone,' Evdokia said, 'she's back now.'

But then Kimya disappeared again. This time she was with a

دوست

group of children of her age just outside the village, watching over the communal flock of goats and sheep. None of the children paid much attention when she ran down the slope after one of the goats that had strayed. That was something they all did in turn. The afternoon was already far advanced when they noticed that Kimya was not with them. They called her name: 'Kimya! Kimya!' It was like a game at first, but only the echo answered them. As they walked back to the village without Kimya, their animals in front of them, they worried. What would Kimya's parents say?

It was several hours later and dark when Kimya finally reappeared. This time Farokh was angry.

'Kimya, this can't go on. We all worry about you, and there you go pretending that everything is as it should be. But it's not.' He was frowning, his voice shaking. 'From now on, I forbid you to go anywhere without your mother; she will keep an eye on you. No more walking by yourself or with the other children! Do you understand?'

Kimya stared at Farokh, silent. She didn't seem to comprehend.

'Well, enough for today,' Evdokia said, and turning towards Kimya, she added, 'Tomorrow you and Aishel will help me with the vegetables.'

## III

EVDOKIA WIPED THE SWEAT FROM HER FOREHEAD. SEVERAL months had gone by since Farokh's outburst and it was now the beginning of summer, and though the afternoon was far advanced, the sun was still high. From the roof terrace where she was standing, she could see the peaks of the mountains in the distance, while down at her feet, spread on a large worn-out rug, the wheat boiled early in the morning had gone hard. She was thinking of Kimya. The child seemed at last to have settled into the daily routine of the village. It was a relief.

She turned back towards the small crowd of women, children and young men gathered on the roof attending the last phase of this wheat ritual which every summer engulfed the village. Armed with a basket, her cousin Anna was pouring the wheat down from as high as she could in order for it to be sifted by the wind. Still a few hours of work, Evdokia thought, then, at last, I'll be able to sit down and enjoy the evening. She joined the others and started to busy herself packing the wheat into the old hemp bags the young men were soon to carry to the storage hut.

And now the work was over. The sun was turning the houses into embers, and streaks of orange and red clouds stretched over the village as it slowly sank into its evening peace. Evdokia reflected that once again the village could relax in the knowledge that next winter it wouldn't starve. Around her the roof was now free for the family to sit together, with only a few grains of wheat left as a reminder of the previous labour. It had been a long day. Her whole body was longing for rest. She went down the wooden ladder and returned with the tray of tea Aishel had prepared. Farokh and the children soon followed and Evdokia sat down and smiled at the sight of her family. Aishel was already pouring the tea and Farokh was puffing at his pipe with Kimya snuggling against him. It was a familiar scene.

Their neighbour Hussein, a devout Muslim, had joined them for the evening. He and Farokh never tired of teasing each other, Hussein scolding Farokh for his lack of attendance at the mosque, with Farokh quick to answer that God's dwelling was far bigger than the four walls of the mosque. At this Hussein replied that, though this might be true, God still liked to have a special place of His own where He could watch His people gathered together.

'Your God is lazy.' Farokh laughed. 'Mine doesn't mind having a look everywhere.'

Evdokia never took part in these battles. Men are such children! Just like their son, Tahir, who looked so handsome in the new green shirt she had made for him. Evdokia looked at him with pride. One day soon, he will marry and give me some grandchildren.

'Baba, tell us again how you met Mama.' Kimya smiled up at her father. 'Was Mama very, very beautiful?'

'You little devil, you know I never tire of telling the story. Yes, your mother was beautiful, as beautiful as a spring flower.' Farokh grinned as he looked at the tired face of his wife.

Kimya curled up more comfortably against him. 'Tell us, Baba, tell us.'

دوست

'Well, I was still a child like you when I arrived in this part of the world with a few other families and their flocks. We didn't live in stone houses then, but in tents made of felt. We followed our goats and sheep through the mountains in search of new pastures, and we never settled for long anywhere. We often pitched our tents on the slopes near a village where we could barter our milk, wool and cheese for vegetables and fruit.' Farokh paused, thinking of his people. 'My ancestors had come from far away in the East,' he said. 'That's what my father once had told me. It was a long time ago, though, before I was born. I myself had never known anywhere other than this land of Rum, ruled, my father said, by a Sultan whose court was in the city of Konya, some five days' walk from this village. At the time, only my uncle and his sons – who were older than me – went to Konya and Laranda, the two cities where they sold our wool and rugs. With the money from the sale they bought knives and cooking pots, and sometimes pretty shawls for our women. My cousins always came back full of stories I found difficult to believe. They talked of buildings made of carved stones, of people speaking strange languages and wearing even stranger dresses. I felt no great desire to see these cities. I loved my life in the mountains – one day here, one day there, never in the same place for very long, with only the sky above our heads as protection.'

Farokh stopped, lost in his thoughts. Funny how he now felt content to live in the village! In a sense, that's where his life as a man had begun.

Kimya waited. She knew not to disturb the sudden silences that fell over Farokh when he talked of the past.

He soon continued: 'One day, my people had set up their camp

12

near this village. I was by then a man of eighteen. I was still watching the family flock and helping with the shearing, but now I was also involved in the sale of the wool and the rugs and I, too, went to Konya and to Laranda. There I saw with my own eyes that my uncle and cousins had not lied. There were many buildings with beautiful carvings. There were mosques decorated with turquoise tiles, and people from all over the world. But I found it overwhelming, even oppressive. Not for me this life of noise and agitation! True, one heard interesting stories there, especially in Konya. People talked of temporary alliances between the Sultan and some Byzantine princes. A merchant told me that around the time of my birth there had been such an alliance with a great Emperor of the West, named after the colour of his red beard. The Sultan had allowed the Christian Emperor to cross these very mountains on his way to Syria and Palestine. And that was not a small thing because the Christian Emperor was leading a mighty army of some hundred and fifty thousand strong men – so the merchant told me. But it was already early summer when the Emperor and his men left Konya. It was hot and these people were not used to such heat.'

For a moment Farokh could almost see the foreign soldiers trudging through the mountain paths in the summer heat. 'Many of them died on the way,' he said, 'and on reaching the other side of the mountains, well, that was the end of them.' Farokh paused, taken by the vision. 'It must have been terrible,' he said. 'Later on people recounted that the red-bearded Emperor was so hot that he had drawn his horse into a river and there he had drowned. What was left of his army disbanded and was never heard of afterwards.'

Kimya interrupted, 'Did the horse drown too?'

13

دوست

Farokh laughed. 'That I don't know. It was a great many years ago, before my family arrived in this land. What I know is that when I came to the village, the people here were still mostly Christian, and so was your mother. We, for our part, were followers of Islam, and with some of my people settling in the villages, mosques were erected, sometimes only a few steps away from the church. There were also villages, like this one, that were too poor to have a mosque built, so we simply used a wing of the church for our prayers. You remember, Evdokia?'

Evdokia nodded. 'Things were changing so fast,' she said. 'It was not always easy.'

Farokh frowned at the memories. 'No, it was not. In some villages there were terrible massacres, sometimes at the hand of my own people. Sometimes it was the Christians coming from the West who killed and plundered. They were on their way, they said, to take back "the holy land". There was even a time when the Western Christians fought the Byzantine Christians until the great city of Constantinople fell into their hands. They slaughtered its inhabitants, and burned and looted the city.' Farokh stared into the night as if the flames were rising in front of his eyes. 'I was still a child then. I remember the fear and contempt in my father's voice when he said, "Christians killing Christians!" But here,' Farokh continued, 'we were lucky. Terrible things were happening all around, but the turmoil hardly ever touched us.'

'But, Baba, tell me. Where was Mama then?'

'I'm coming to it. Wait!' Farokh cleared his throat and then continued. 'Often when I went to the village, I entered the church. I knew this was where Isa, the great prophet of the Christians, and his mother Maryam were venerated. I liked to sit in the dark near the altar on the right, and watch the Virgin and her child.'

Kimya looked up at Farokh. She too visited the church at times and liked to sit in front of the Virgin.

'But,' Farokh went on, 'there was something I didn't like in the church. That was the man nailed to a cross on the main altar. The Virgin and her child welcomed me. But why, in a place of such peace, was there a tortured body for all to see? I still can't understand. You see, we knew what was happening then in the great cities of Central Asia at the hand of the Mongols and the sight of this man bleeding on his cross was too much a reminder of those horrors. My people, too, like the Mongols, came from the steppes and the deserts where such cities as Herat, Balkh and Samarkand had risen. But instead of destroying them, my people learned from them and shared their own craftsmanship and knowledge with them.'

Farokh fell silent. He was thinking of his people: he was proud of them. They had brought with them their new faith in a God of mercy and compassion. Their places of prayer had the flavour of the vast expanses of land his ancestors had roamed. The mosques he had entered in Konya and Laranda had the unaltered austerity of the desert, their only ornament the geometrical patterns endlessly repeated on the walls, like, he thought, the breath of men repeating the name of God. And yet, he had to admit, whenever I go to the new mosque in the village, I miss the presence of the Virgin and her child.

Kimya was becoming impatient. 'And Mama,' she asked. 'How did you meet her?'

'Just wait. I'm coming to it.' Farokh took a sip from his tea, now cold. 'One morning – the sun had just risen above the mountain ridge – I once again entered the church and there, in front of the Virgin, I saw a girl on her knees. She was so absorbed in her prayers that she didn't notice me coming in. I left the church on tiptoe. Outside I sat on a stone and, I don't know why, I waited for her. It was spring. The air was still crisp, but it held a promise of warmth. Soon the girl emerged from the church. She looked at me and I had just enough time to catch the green of her eyes before she walked away. I followed her at a distance, hardly aware of what I was doing, until she disappeared into one of the stone houses. The following day I found myself passing in front of her house with my flock, and as I was wondering whether I would ever see her again, there she was standing on the doorstep, a hint of a smile in her eyes.' Farokh looked at his wife.

'You were wearing a dark blue skirt and an embroidered blouse,' he said.

Evdokia nodded. 'Yes, I remember.' It seemed such a long time ago!

Farokh continued, 'I wanted to smile back at her, but instead I stopped and stared until the smile in her eyes vanished. She had very pale skin, like you,' Farokh said, patting Kimya's cheek. 'I remember the sun shining on a curl of red-gold hair that had slipped from under your scarf,' he said, looking at his wife. 'How beautiful, I thought. Then I heard a woman's voice calling, 'Evdokia, Evdokia, where are you?' and you turned away and disappeared through the door. That night, while lying under the stars, unable to sleep, I repeated your name several times.

'Every day now my animals were taking me closer to the houses.

دوست

One day I saw her with a group of girls picking vegetables in a patch of land on the southern slope down towards the village. Some days later I saw her again with her friends, this time collecting the little green plums that grow around the village. They all started laughing at me, and for a while I didn't dare to go near the houses again. Then one day, at the spring outside the village, we met once more. As always she was with a group of other girls. She was carrying a heavy earthen jug and, before I could think, I had the jug in my hands and started to fill it up. I gave it back to her and for a second our hands touched. I felt my face burning and I quickly collected my animals and walked away.

'Then, there was that summer morning! It still feels as if it were yesterday. Down in the village, as every summer, the women were washing great bulks of wheat at the fountain. The water was rushing down, red with earth; some of the women were sifting tiny stones from the grain. Their voices resounded in the morning air. From where I stood, they were like patches of colour. I wondered if she was among them. For a few minutes, I forgot all about my sheep and goats, and allowed my heart to long for the sight of the girl with green eyes.

' "Is this how you watch your animals?" Her voice was full of laughter. Startled, I turned round and saw in front of me the very girl who was haunting my thoughts.

' "Your goats are straying; shall I help you?"

'I couldn't think and I must have looked rather silly.

' "I came to ask you if you could bring us some milk later on. I brought you some turnips and peas, and also a few plums."

'Her voice was firm and clear. She was so at ease, so light. I, for

17

دوست

my part, felt heavy, like a lump of clay before being turned into a fine jug. Fortunately the thought made me laugh and, thank God, I relaxed.

'"Wait," I said, and I ran after my goats that were scattered all around and gathered them back. Then to my astonishment I heard myself asking, "Tell me about Isa and His mother in the church."

'The smile in her eyes had vanished. She looked suddenly serious, almost solemn. "Mary, the Virgin? She protects us all; she is all compassion and her son – we call Him Jesus – is all love."

'She was standing there in front of me, as clear and fresh as spring water, I thought. Around us, the leaves in the trees were rustling as if in approval.

'"I'm going to marry you," I said. And I was amazed at my certainty. Again the words had surged up without my willing them. Something like the shadow of a smile had reappeared in her eyes.

'"You must ask my father first," she said. "Come tonight."

'And before turning away, she added, "And don't forget the milk."

'I stood, dazed, watching her as she walked off towards the village. I could hear the stones rolling down under her feet, and again the voices of the women around the fountain. What had happened? Something important, something decisive, like when you decide to go one way and not the other at a crossroads. But I, myself, had not decided anything! Somehow it had all happened without me, and yet I had never felt so free and all I could do was to praise God.'

Once again Farokh fell silent. That moment was still so clear in his mind. At the time, he remembered, an old song he had heard his grandfather sing had come to his lips, as vast as the sky, as vast as the mountain ranges around. 'The world was mine,' he said, 'and I was the happiest man in the world.'

'Baba, Baba.' Kimya's voice was pressing. 'What did Grandpa say when you went to ask him?'

'Ah,' Farokh sighed. 'It was not easy. It was early evening and everything around us was engulfed in golden light.'

'Were you afraid, Baba?'

'Yes, I was. But I was also determined. Evdokia's father was sitting outside on the stone bench near the door. He watched me approach and I could see he was weighing me up from head to toe.

'I'm going to marry your daughter, I was telling myself while walking towards the old man. I'm going to marry her. But once in front of him, I couldn't utter a word. Your grandpa was sitting very straight and his eyes seemed to see through me. I felt like a child found out. He looked so severe. Where was all my strength and determination? My legs felt weak and my heart was full of fear. Why should this man give me his daughter? He had a house; I had only a tent made of goat hair. He had some land of his own; I had the whole mountain slopes to roam, but couldn't claim any part of them as my own. And, worst of all, these people were Christians; their prophet was Isa, and they worshipped His mother, Maryam. My family had recently converted to the faith of Islam, that is, surrender to Allah, the one and only God, and His prophet was Mohammed. How could we reconcile our differences? A wave of despair overwhelmed me. Evdokia could never be mine. Her father, this man in brown garb, would laugh at me if I even dared tell him of my insane desire.

دوست

' "Well, young man, what brings you here?"

' "Your daughter," I finally managed to say, "your daughter has asked me to bring you some milk." And I showed him the jug of fresh milk I was holding.

'At that moment I noticed the lines at the corners of his eyes. They seemed to have multiplied and around his mouth two lines had appeared. Undoubtedly the face in front of me was smiling.

' "Is that all?" Evdokia's father asked me, and I could see there was a twinkle in his eyes. "My daughter told me you wanted to ask me something; then ask."

'I couldn't believe what I had just heard. Was this really happening? Then the words I had repeated to myself while walking towards Evdokia's house burst out of my mouth: "I'm going to marry your daughter," I said, then stopped. This was no asking! How could I have uttered such a thing? This time, I really had lost all my chances of being accepted. But to my astonishment, Grandpa was now laughing with all his heart.

' "Oh, my son, you need some practice with your manners. Do you not? This is what I call being straightforward. And how do you know that my daughter will accept you as a husband?"

'His question took me aback. Had she changed her mind? Had she not mentioned me to her father after all? Perhaps I shouldn't have come. I was going to turn and run away when the old man held up his hand.

' "You're like a wild horse, my friend. Calm down and sit here with me."

'I did as I was told. My mind was in turmoil.

' "So you want to marry my daughter," the old man said.

دوست

"Evdokia will make a good wife, you know. She has her own character, though, but I can see that you know what you want and that you are ready to take risks."

'For a while we remained silent. The last rays of the sun brushed Grandpa's face, and he looked as if he were made of gold.

' "There is one condition," he said, breaking the silence, and I felt my heart sink. Was he about to ask me to go and bring back some treasure hidden at the bottom of the sea, or the heart of some dreadful beast waiting to devour anyone who dared to get too close? Instead I heard something I was not prepared for.

' "I want you to settle here in this village," Evdokia's father said. "We need new blood, and also" – he was now grinning – "I want to see my grandchildren grow up."

'And this,' Farokh concluded, 'is how you came to be born here in your mother's village.' He looked at Kimya huddled against him, but she was fast asleep. Evdokia was shaking her head.

'You forgot to mention that my father made you build a house before allowing our wedding to take place, and that it took you six months, six months,' she repeated with a tone of reproach in her voice, 'before we could at last be married.'

Farokh laughed, his wide embracing laugh that made him look larger than life. 'You will never forgive me, will you?' he said, still laughing.

Evdokia was shaking her head, trying hard not to smile.

21

## IV

THE DAY HAD STARTED LIKE ANY OTHER DAY. AHMED HAD GONE to work at the small office where he spent hours writing legal documents for the *qadi*, mainly about land tenures and rights of access to properties, and though the afternoon was still not far advanced he had finished his workload for the day. His thoughts turned towards Jalal ud din, the man people called Maulana, Our Master. Maulana was the son of another teacher, Baha ud din Walad, now dead, and, like his father, he taught at the main college in Konya, the *madrassa*, where he also preached almost every afternoon to anyone who cared to attend. Some of Ahmed's friends said he was not arrogant and dull like so many other teachers, that on the contrary he was warm and kind. Others complained that he accepted Christians and Jews, and even women among his disciples. Certainly that was wrong, wasn't it? The gossip left Ahmed indifferent, but none the less until that day he had always found an excuse not to go and listen to Maulana.

I do my prayers, I go to the mosque on Friday, I give alms, what need have I to go and listen to a preacher? There were too many of them anyway. Not only the Christian monks who tried to stem the rise of Islam, or the Franks on their way to Palestine, but all those beggars in disguise who came from the East and made their living from swallowing swords, spitting fire, or pretending to read the

دوست

future. True, Ahmed didn't think the son of Baha ud din Walad was one of those, though Baha ud din had also come from the East. Everybody knew that Baha ud din was a great religious teacher whom the Sultan Ala ud din Kaykobad had invited to come and settle in Konya with his family. Many said that Baha ud din's son, Jalal, was even greater than his father. No, it was not suspicion that kept Ahmed away, it was more the vague feeling that Maulana might reach somewhere in him where he, Ahmed, didn't really want to look.

That day, however, the thought of Jalal ud din preaching at his college was insistent. After all, what have I to fear? And, putting ink and paper aside, Ahmed set off towards the *madrassa*. As he came nearer, he started to walk faster as if in fear of missing an important appointment. Why this haste? I'm only going to listen to the words of a religious teacher.

The doors of the *madrassa* were wide open when he arrived, the hall spilling over with people. Ahmed pushed his way to the front row among half-whispered curses, but all he heard were words that burned anew in his heart.

'He is the Creator and the Provider; to Him all things shall return.'

Standing on a small platform and facing the crowd, a man dressed in a blue robe was speaking words that brought tears to his eyes.

'Love for the Creator is latent in all the world and in all men, be they Magians, Jews or Christians.'

Ahmed wiped the perspiration from his forehead.

23

دوست

'Whosoever fears God, even though he be an infidel, is religious, not irreligious.'

His head was spinning. Thoughts he had never entertained assaulted him like flames leaping out of fire. What am I doing in Konya? What am I doing filling in meaningless pieces of paper day after day? The fear was back, fierce, yet strangely mixed with joy. I am already twenty-two and what have I accomplished? Nothing! Only the words he was hearing made sense, the rest was entertainment. I can't go on wasting my life. The thought was already pushing him out of the hall.

He was now walking towards the house he shared with his brother Osman, on the outskirts of the city. Two years before, their parents had died, and the house was left empty most of the day. Caught in its afternoon nap, it looked asleep when he arrived. In full blossom, the old apricot tree was gently swaying in the breeze.

Rapidly he collected a few shirts and a kaftan, pushed the lot into a bag and threw his winter coat over his shoulder. He then sat down and scribbled a note on a piece of parchment.

'Osman, my dear brother, don't be aggrieved by my decision. Maulana, may he be blessed, has saved me from myself. I am leaving Konya to go and live in solitude. I'm heading to the mountains where, God willing, I'll find peace and meaning. Your loving brother, Ahmed.'

He left the note in evidence and, without looking back, walked towards the heart of the city. It would soon be dusk, that time of day when life in the bazaar came to a sudden crescendo as if to compensate for the slumber of the night to come. Rapidly he passed the

دوست

carpet shops and their piles of rugs, many of which had come from
Damascus or Cilicia. He caught sight of a pale blue and cream
prayer rug made of silk such as Konya was famous for. The smell of
burned wood and horses' manure, mixed with those of saffron,
pepper and cardamom, was overwhelming. It brought back the
memory of that day when he had gone to see his brother who was
working nearby in a warehouse behind the caravanserai of the
cloth merchants. Osman's work consisted of sorting out the various
goods the caravans brought from Herat, Samarkand, Bokhara, and
many other great cities of the East. There he had watched Osman
stacking huge bundles of silk wrapped in cotton cloth next to piles
of carpets still dusty from their journey. He had looked at the many
boxes of fine porcelain that were waiting to be loaded on to horses,
some to go straight to the palace, others to Constantinople, and
others still to the port of Attaleia in the south where, Osman said,
Venetian ships were waiting to carry them away.

But today Ahmed had no time for all this, and no desire to see
his brother. Walking on, he soon entered the goldsmiths' quarter and
for a second he stopped, arrested by the sight of the glittering
goblets, trays and ewers caught in the sunlight that filtered through
the lattice. Ahmed looked at the richly engraved sheaths on display,
no doubt hiding some fine blades. I will need one of these, he
thought. But I have no need for such luxury. Already the merchant
was on the doorstep.

'These have just arrived from Aleppo, would you like to see
them? Look at this one; isn't it a beauty?' The polished blade shone
like a mirror out of its engraved silver sheath. 'This dagger will last
you for ever.'

دوست

For a second, Ahmed was tempted. 'No,' he finally said. 'I need something simpler; just a good knife will do.'

The merchant sighed and pulled a large knife out of a simple leather sheath. 'This will be your friend for many long years,' he said, and Ahmed nodded.

'Yes, this is what I need. How much?'

'Seventy-five dirhams, a very good price.'

Ahmed handed him the money without bargaining, to the disappointment of the man who grumbled that nowadays people had no manners.

Paying no attention to the merchant's muttering, Ahmed walked off, heading towards the food market that stretched over several lanes on his left. Bursting to the rim, the usual hemp bags of grains, flour and nuts of all sorts sat next to small pyramids of black olives and white squares of cheese. Half hidden in the darkness, smaller bags of dried apricots and prunes leaned against the huge oil jars that kept guard at the back of the shops.

Ahmed had already made up his mind. All he needed was a bundle of bread, some nuts and dried fruit, a few handfuls of olives and a piece of cheese. That will keep me going for a while; then I will get provisions from the villages. Once in the mountains I will live off my hunting, at least to begin with. A strange exaltation had taken hold of him. This is the beginning. I'm starting, at last. 'You are starting what?' said a mocking voice inside him. He laughed. I'm starting to live; I was half asleep, now I'm alive.

'It's good to see you in such happy mood, Ahmed.'

There in front of him, his hands packed with notebooks as usual, stood his old friend Theophanes, with whom he had been

26

دوست

taught to read and write by an old Christian monk. At the time Ahmed was already versed in Persian, the language of his family and of the court, while Theophanes, the son of a Greek notary, was more advanced in the language of Byzantium. The two boys had helped each other in their studies. Theophanes – dark eyes and blond hair: Ahmed – grey eyes and dark hair. 'Greek and Persian blood,' people used to remark when they saw them together. 'True citizens of Konya.' He smiled back at his friend while the thought crossed his mind that in his new life, if he ever spoke, it would be a mixture of Greek and that new language that was infiltrating Konya more and more, the language of the Turkomans. Why are men so different? As if answering his question, the words of Maulana came back, insistent: 'Love for the Creator is latent in all men.'

'Ahmed, are you dreaming? And what are you doing with your winter coat?' Theophanes was not one to accept some evasive answer.

Ahmed hesitated, embarrassed. How could he who gloried at being what he called 'sensible', explain that his life had been turned upside down by the words of a religious teacher, however famous this teacher might be? 'I'm leaving,' Ahmed said. 'I can't stay here any more; this life is over.'

'You ... what?' Theophanes was staring at Ahmed, half laughing, half suspicious. 'You are leaving,' he repeated. 'Why? Where to?' Theophanes was now alarmed.

'Look, Theophanes, I know we are friends, but I am not the same person I was only yesterday, even just this morning.' How could he make his friend understand, when he, himself, could not make sense of what was happening to him? He looked at Theophanes helplessly, feeling suddenly sad, then shook himself. 'It was good knowing you,' he said awkwardly. 'Perhaps our paths will cross again.' The words felt absurd and he turned away brusquely. He heard his friend calling his name, but he was already lost in the crowd.

Soon he reached the main gate of the city. Poor Theophanes, but what else could I do? He pressed on, past the two fortified walls and the watchtower, then crossed the *maidan*, where he had so much enjoyed riding with his friends. Half of the *maidan* was now covered with the tents of the newly arrived refugees. Far in the distance the blue line of the Taurus was calling.

How many days had now gone by since his departure from Konya? Ahmed had lost count. One day followed another: one moment he was climbing a hill covered with firs, the next he was descending into a valley shaded with birches and oaks. One moment he found himself engulfed in shadow at the bottom of a gully, the next he was walking with the sun beaming at him through the trees.

One late afternoon, after a steep walk, as he stood on a ledge, tired but exhilarated by the fresh air, great gusts of wind swirling around him, he faced a sky ablaze, with the red disc of the sun sinking fast behind the mountain ranges. Around him the trees, the rocks were glowing, and for a moment he was filled with a sense of glory mingled with gratitude. Then he shivered. It was still early spring and the air was colder than in Konya. A sudden pang of nostalgia hit him. In that city where he had spent the whole twenty-two years of his life, there were always minarets and spires shaping the sky, and the sound and throb of men's activity. Here, everything was green with patches of blue and purple, and the only sounds were the blowing of the wind and the cries of the birds. It was both magnificent and overwhelming. But why should he regret his life in Konya? He thought of his daily routine in the *qaḍi's* shop, the noise, the dust, the bitter quarrels between merchants and landowners, all this – he now laughed – because they were afraid of losing what they had, or wanted to have more than they had. This is all over, he told himself, and his regret gave place to a sense of relief.

At that moment, the sound of running water caught his ear, reminding him that he was thirsty and it was time to eat. His supper would be simple, though, as he had only one piece of bread left to eat. Tomorrow I must find a village. But for the time being all he needed was to find somewhere for the night. He followed the sound of the water and soon discovered, half hidden under the thickets, a stream rushing over a bed of rocks. He ate his bread, washed and, having performed his prayers, wrapped himself in his coat and lay down on the thick cover of leaves.

As sleep slowly took hold of him, he remembered his first night away from home. It seemed a long time ago. That night he had slept in an orchard along the road, and as he lay down for the night he had addressed a silent prayer somewhere above the trees: 'O You who are everywhere, please send Your angels to protect me from the wild animals.' He had quickly corrected himself: 'One angel will be enough. I wouldn't disturb the heavens for such a small request.' The next morning a cold wetness on his face woke him up. On opening his eyes he just had enough time to glimpse a ball of red fur climbing up the birch tree beside his head. 'Yes, yes,' he grumbled, 'I know it's time to pray.' Then he laughed. 'I asked to be protected from wild

دوست

animals. Didn't I? Not from squirrels.'

After that, as the old Roman road narrowed into a path heading towards the Taurus and there were no more orchards, he had taken shelter in caves. Once he had tried the hollow of a tree, but in the morning his body ached, and he decided a bed of dead leaves would suit him better.

He was still laughing at the memory of that first night among the trees when he finally fell asleep. When he woke up, the birds were sending their first messages to the coming light. He spread his coat on the ground, poured some water out of his gourd and, having done his ablutions, he faced towards the east and gathered himself. The words he had heard in Konya only a few days ago – or was it weeks? – kept haunting him. 'He is the Creator and the Provider. To Him all things shall return.' He heard them in the wind, in the chattering of the birds, in the light filtering through the leaves, and was overcome by a feeling of gratitude. A new glorious day was facing him. Amazing how he felt so at home in these woods! The cracking of a branch, the ruffling of the trees, the sudden flight of a bird, all these sounds were now part of his life. He went back to the escarpment where, the previous evening, he had watched the sunset, and stretched. High in the blue of the sky over the valley, a hawk was gliding. He suddenly caught the sound of women's high-pitched voices in the distance. They seemed to be coming from the other side of the valley and reverberated against the cliff on which he stood. There was no trace of a village, though. It must be hidden behind the trees, he thought. It was time to go and get some food. Wrapping his coat around himself, he threw his bag over his shoulder and started to walk down in the direction of the voices.

# – V –

THE FIRST THING THAT CAUGHT AHMED'S EYES AS HE STOOD IN front of the row of poplars, which seemed to mark the limit of the village, were the two shapes a few yards away. They were blurred by the steam that rose from a large cauldron beside them. Armed with wooden bats, they were beating the piles of clothes folded in front of them. A young girl pushed a bundle of twigs under the cauldron and almost immediately small orange flames licked its flanks. A few steps above, a little crowd of women and children were gathered around a fountain where, one after the other, they filled their pitchers. Behind them, a group of boys on their donkeys were waiting, ready to carry the heavier jugs, while a few children, shouting excitedly, ran around splashing each other. A goat crossed over the path, sending a couple of hens flying in protest. There was something soothing about the whole scene, he thought, one that must be repeating itself in every village at this time of day when the air still carries the coldness of the night and the sun has not yet risen from behind the mountains.

'The spring is early this year,' one of the women said, looking at the sky where a flock of starlings was flying over.

'That's true,' said another. 'Soon we'll have some fresh vegetables. I'm tired of eating bulgur and beans.'

A child ran towards one of the women washing the clothes and

31

pulled at her skirt. She pointed at Ahmed. The two women stopped in their task and looked up. He imagined them frowning as they tried to see through the steam. The group of women and children around the fountain had fallen silent. *Of course, these people aren't used to seeing strangers. To them I probably mean danger just as much as news.* He started to walk slowly towards them and they drew back, leaving an empty space between him and the fountain. *I must look pretty awful with my hair and beard uncombed, and my eyes aching and red,* he thought.

'*Salam aleikoum*,' he said, with a smile he hoped was engaging. He saw the women relax.

'*Aleikoum salam*,' they replied automatically.

'My name is Ahmed.' Taking a gourd out of his bag, he indicated that he wanted to fill it up.

The children were still clinging to their mothers. One of them, a boy in a bright orange kaftan, ventured, 'Where do you come from?'

'From Konya. Have you heard of Konya?'

The boy nodded, while the women whispered to each other, 'He comes from Konya. He comes from Konya.'

'Where are you travelling to?'

Ahmed looked down at the young girl who had stepped closer. She had bright dark eyes, shadowed by long curled eyelashes. He was amused. *She seemed so serious and she was so pretty!*

'Are you going to Damascus?' the child insisted, as though she herself had travelled the world.

'Kimya, be quiet,' one of the women said.

But it was clear that all of them were waiting for his answer. For a moment, Ahmed hesitated. Only He knows that I am not really going anywhere, though He knows, too, that my life in Konya is over. 'There is nowhere to go,' he finally answered with a sigh. 'He is nowhere and He is everywhere.'

The women stared at him, perplexed, then shrugged.

Ahmed shrugged too. Why should they understand? Even to his best friend he had been unable to make sense of his sudden need for solitude. The young girl was watching him with a curious look on her face, intense and remote at the same time. So her name was Kimya. He was looking at her when she became still as though listening to some distant call. Ahmed noticed the fear in the eyes of the woman who seemed to be her mother. Then the child came back to herself and the woman relaxed. It had all happened very quickly, as when a cloud passes in front of the sun then moves away. The child was now observing him with attention.

'You will need some food,' she said matter-of-factly and Ahmed laughed. He could almost hear his own mother. 'You're going to need some food, my son.'

'You're absolutely right. But I'm a good hunter.' And out of his bag he pulled the small rabbit he had caught the previous night. 'Would you give me some cheese and bread for this?' he asked, now addressing her mother.

Evdokia took the rabbit in her hands, examined it and without a word started to walk away, indicating that he was to follow.

He liked her. She looked strong, her face furrowed like ploughed earth. She had that innate dignity villagers wear as kings wear their crowns or old men their wisdom. They are lucky, he thought. The earth, the rain and the wind are their constant companions and, like them, they may be fierce and violent at times, but they are true and unpretentious.

He followed the woman, Kimya by his side. As he walked, he became aware that his feet were aching.

He was sitting on a low stone bench placed against the wall of the house which, a few minutes earlier, Kimya and her mother had entered. The sun was now high and he stretched, enjoying the warmth.

I've almost arrived, he thought. That surprised him. Already he was making plans: he would build himself a hut somewhere in the woods, not far away, and he would settle there, his life free of unnecessary concerns. These last days of walking in solitude had cleared his mind. He felt cleaner, simpler. The worries that used to weigh on him had dropped away. Being early or late had lost all meaning. Deciding to be here rather than there made no sense. Now is always here. The thought made him laugh, and his laughter rippled through the children who had gathered in front of him. At that moment Kimya came out of the house holding a small bundle wrapped in a blue piece of cloth.

'This is for you,' she said, handing him the small parcel. 'Be careful, there are eggs.'

'Thank you.' He took the parcel and stood up. 'I'll be on my way now.'

She watched him with the same seriousness she had shown earlier. 'You will come again?' This was hardly a question.

'God will tell,' he said and she nodded.

As he entered the woods Ahmed turned back and looked at the

village. Everything and everyone is where it should be. This village and its people had their place in his life, just as the now familiar sounds of the forest welcoming him. Overcome by a wave of gratitude, he fell on his knees and once again he laughed. 'O You, the Merciful, You have even provided a cushion of leaves for my comfort.'

# – VI –

I T WAS NOW SEVERAL WEEKS SINCE THE STRANGER HAD appeared at the edge of the forest and, in so doing, provided new material for the women's gossip: how long was he going to stay? What would he do in the winter? How extraordinary that he was from Konya! Some of their men had been there, after all. They had told them of the riches that came to Konya from all over the world, of the Christians, Muslims and Jews who lived there at peace with each other. But this man didn't look rich, and as for his religion, that was not of great concern to them. Not so long ago, when the village had no mosque of its own, the eastern corner of the church had been used for the Muslim prayer on Friday. True, at the time some of the Christians had complained that this was an insult to the God of Isa and Maryam. But Evdokia had remarked that her husband venerated the Holy Virgin just as much as she, a Christian, did, and that anyway she was sure God the father and Allah were good friends. To which Farokh had added that if there was only one God, as the imam as well as their priest kept telling them, then He certainly didn't mind being worshipped in more than one way. But of course, Farokh couldn't do things like everybody else. He hardly ever went to the mosque or the church; instead he never failed to bow to the new moon or to pour a few drops of water on the ground before drinking.

36

دوست

'This is the earth's share,' he had once explained. 'My parents and my grandparents did this as an offering to the gods.' And he talked of the shamans his ancestors feared and revered. 'When I was a child, there was a small idol pinned up at the head of our tent. It was made of fabric; it was dark and worn out. In those times before drinking,' he said, 'the head of the family always sprinkled water over the idol. When we all became Muslim, the idol disappeared, but the sprinkling of water remained.'

Unaware of the turmoil his presence was causing, Ahmed had settled in a small cave two hours' walk north of the village. Tahir had caught sight of him one day while collecting wood. The man had made a sign indicating he wanted to be left alone. Later on Tahir saw him prostrated in front of the cave. When told, the women agreed: a holy man near their village was a good omen. The imam was consulted. 'Should we take him some food?' He approved and baskets of vegetables and fruit found their way to Ahmed's cave to be left at the entrance.

Father Chrisostom, too, who visited the village every fourth moon, had been told about Ahmed. 'What do you think of such a way of life? Is it right?'

His answer was cautious. 'It depends. To live in solitude is not for everyone; it's only for a very few.'

Father Chrisostom's parish covered a dozen small villages scattered over the valleys and peaks of the Taurus Mountains. 'You need good legs to be a village priest,' he used to say with a large smile, which made the wrinkles around his eyes deepen, at the same time hiding the weariness he felt creeping into his bones. One day I will be too old for this work, he had been thinking recently, and then

دوست

what will happen to these people? He worried. They still have their
children baptised, but they are building mosques and they let their
churches become dilapidated. The new religion of Islam was gaining
ground, it couldn't be denied. In Constantinople the bishops met and
talked, but nothing came of it, and Father Chrisostom sighed: this
work that had shaped his whole life, in the end what would it have
achieved?

'I tell you, it's wrong for a young man to keep away from the world
and not to father children.' As they did every morning the women
were filling their jugs at the fountain, and once again they were
talking about Ahmed.

'It's all very well to be a holy man,' old Anya was grumbling, 'but
what is wrong with being both holy and a father? Look at our
imam.'

'And look at Father Chrisostom,' interjected Evdokia.

'Well, Father Chrisostom says that God wants His children to
multiply,' Safia proclaimed with a triumphant voice.

Evdokia burst into laughter. 'Oh, Safia, you're certainly doing
God's will; already five children, another one on its way, and you're
just over twenty!'

Safia proudly held her protruding belly. 'Children are the seeds
of the future,' she said sententiously, repeating the words of Father
Chrisostom.

There was something rather comical, Evdokia thought, about
the whole village discussing marriage and childbearing because of
a young hermit who clearly had no interest in any of it.

After a time, however, people lost interest. Oh, they didn't forget

دوست

Ahmed, no; rather he was now part of the surroundings, an undeniable presence, like the forest, or the stream at the bottom of the village. The land needed water and weeding, and Ahmed in his cave needed regular feeding, but he was not a curiosity any more. Once a week a child left a basket of food at the entrance to the cave and sometimes a bird or a hare came back in return. Whenever Ahmed was in sight, he made it clear that he didn't want to talk, and this was accepted just as it was accepted that the sun rose in the east and streams ran down the slopes.

What mattered today was not Ahmed, however, but the arrival of Father Chrisostom after more than three months of absence. The villagers were not always clear as to their allegiance to the Church, but they were clear enough about their affection for the priest, and his visits always brought a festive mood to the village.

This evening the women would light candles in the church, the new babies would be dressed in their best clothes, and a mass would be celebrated. Afterwards Father Chrisostom would be invited to share a meal on a roof terrace with some of the families. A fire would be lit and as always his friend the imam would be present. The two men acknowledged their differences in faith, but, through the years, their shared concern for the well-being of the villagers had partly obscured these differences. They were well aware, too, that in the hierarchy of their respective religions their positions differed. The imam was only the leader of the Friday prayer, while Father Chrisostom was an official representative of God, something that, he had to admit, at times weighed heavily on his shoulders. But even this didn't infringe on the warmth of their

دوست

feelings for each other.

Now, sitting by the glow of the roof-top fire, lulled by the buzzing of the conversations around him, Father Chrisostom sank into his thoughts. In the end, he reflected, our differences, either in rank or in convictions, do not matter much in the eyes of God. This opinion, however, he carefully kept to himself. His bishop, he knew, would not appreciate it. But then what did bishops know of the life of these people, busy as they were with their own quarrels as to whether the Latin or the Eastern Church should rule in Constantinople? What did they know of the hardship villagers suffered: the unpredictability of the seasons and, worse, the constant invasions, the passage of troops, the enslavement, the massacres? When I look at these people, when I listen to them, I know they are children of God, and I know this is the only thing that matters. But then, Father Chrisostom agonised, what kind of priest am I? And you, my Lord Jesus, am I forgetting to be Your witness? More than ever he felt the years weighing on him as the new faith of Islam seemed to bring unbearable questions.

'Father, you must not be sad.' The voice interrupting his thoughts was the voice of a child. 'We are so happy to have you with us.'

This was Kimya, of course. This child sees everything, he thought. There is something slightly disquieting about her, difficult to define. Yet she is so lovable.

Kimya was looking at the priest with a quiet gravity. 'I've done all the writing,' she said proudly. 'The whole page. Would you like to see it?'

'Of course I would.'

Whenever he visited the village, Father Chrisostom spent time

دوست

teaching the children how to read and write. Increasingly, they were using words borrowed from the Turkoman nomads, and he felt it his duty to protect as well as he could the Greek language which, after all, had been spoken in these lands for centuries. Sometimes he wondered, however. Was this another lost battle? It seemed no one cared much about languages; languages were simply tools people used. In the cities Arabic and Persian mingled with Greek, but on a more equal basis. Here, it was different: Islam and the language of the Turkomans were slowly supplanting Christianity and the Greek language. How unsettling it was at times to live in this land of Anatolia and the Taurus, pulled between the Byzantine and Persian empires!

And it didn't help that those empires were both threatened on their flanks by barbarians whose 'exploits' were just as horrific whoever perpetrated them – the Turkomans in the east or the Franks and their allies in the west. And now, with the advance of the Mongols, Father Chrisostom reflected, it was not only the individual who was threatened, but whole ways of life with their unique forms and richness. One heard of libraries disappearing in blazes, of illuminated manuscripts torn to pieces, of works of art reduced to rubble. Our world is in turmoil, the old priest sighed, and yet life never ceases. The old are left to their memories while the young build new worlds. Father Chrisostom had not been to Konya for years, but he had heard that, under the enlightened rule of the Sultan, a new culture inspired by Persia, yet not cut off from its Greek roots, had emerged with an art, a style and a beauty of its own. Why do I worry? he thought. God has His own plan, and who are we to question it?

دوست

He was interrupted in his thoughts by a wild, passionate song that rose from the night. The voice was harsh, the sounds hoarse, guttural. The priest couldn't understand the words, but the song had the flavour of horse rides, of deserts and of endless skies. He wondered, Does this belong to the new or the old? The song spiralled up, calling to the Infinite. It was Farokh's voice.

This is prayer, real prayer, Father Chrisostom thought, and once again he felt assailed by doubts. People have their faiths and God hears each one of them. Who are we to tell them how to talk to Him? Never had Farokh sung with such passion, such longing. The man is in pain, but such pain is a call, Father Chrisostom reflected, and that kind of call never stays unanswered. Yet it can take a long time before one is able to hear the answer.

'Father, will you look at my writing?' The voice was imploring.

Startled, he passed his hand over his brow and stared at Kimya still standing beside him. I must be getting old. For a moment he had completely forgotten her. He noticed that Farokh had stopped singing. 'I'm sorry, Kimya. Yes, show me.'

She gave him the piece of paper he had left her almost four months ago with words carefully written for her to copy. Under each of the words he had originally written with a quill, her own writing in charcoal looked heavier but just as precise.

'This is very good, Kimya.' Father Chrisostom smiled. He was pleased. He knew too well that to the villagers his writing lessons were only a curiosity, something that kept the children quiet for a while. Life was harsh in the villages and there were other tasks more pressing than writing, like harvesting the wheat, feeding the animals, irrigating the land, picking the fruit, repairing the roofs before winter. Writing was a luxury for people who could afford servants, not for people like them.

'What are we to do with this child?' The priest started. Farokh, his song now over, was standing in front of him, looking at the sheet of paper with the black signs on it, which meant nothing to him. He was scratching his head and looked puzzled. 'She is not like the others,' he said finally. 'Her mother and I, we worry.'

The priest gave the piece of paper back to Kimya. 'Kimya, your father and I need to talk. I'll give you some new letters before I go.'

She ran towards her mother. 'Look, the father says my letters are very good.'

Father Chrisostom turned to Farokh. 'You should not worry, Farokh. God has His ways, unknown to us.'

Farokh sat down heavily beside the priest.

Father Chrisostom noticed that Farokh's hair was growing white at the sides. 'How old are you, Farokh?'

'How old?' Farokh repeated. He hesitated. 'Almost forty, I imagine. My people didn't keep that kind of record, so nobody really knows.'

'Well, when I married you, some eighteen years ago,' the priest reflected, 'you were about twenty, so you're not far off, you must be in your late thirties.'

Silence fell between the two men, each one lost in his thoughts. In front of them the fire was crackling. From time to time a spark jumped out as if trying to escape.

'A good age,' the priest said after a while.

Night had fallen and above them the sky was like a dark piece of silk studded with tiny diamonds.

دوست

Father Chrisostom returned to the subject that troubled Farokh. 'You're right,' he acknowledged. 'Kimya is different.' And he added, surprised at his own suggestion, 'Perhaps she should go to Konya and study there.' It sounded like a good idea. These people had no money, and it was not rare for young children to be adopted so that they could be provided with an education. There were also convents, and he knew of two, at least, where the child, through his recommendation, would be easily accepted. He was still thinking, unaware that Farokh was now standing in front of him, his face red with anger.

'Send Kimya away?' he burst out. 'Never!'

'I'm not saying this is the thing to do,' Father Chrisostom said in a conciliatory voice, 'but it's something you might want to consider.'

'There is nothing to consider,' Farokh replied and he walked away brusquely.

But Father Chrisostom knew the man. Farokh would first share his anger with his wife, and Evdokia was a wise woman. She would listen to her husband, the imam would be consulted, and in the end the idea would make its way through the village and a consensus would be reached. And if it is right, God will find the way to make it happen. In the meantime, Farokh would let his anger brew, and for a while Father Chrisostom would be the villain. The thought made him smile, and when he felt a hand slip into his, he was not surprised to find Kimya sitting next to him and smiling back at him.

## VII

THE FESTIVITIES WERE OVER AND THE VILLAGE WAS NOW returning to its daily routine. Father Chrisostom had left at dawn, accompanied by Tahir who hoped to find a new blade for the plough in the next village. On the roof terrace Aishel, armed with a bundle of reeds, was sweeping away the shells of sunflower seeds left from last night's gathering.

'Kimya, will you move? Don't you see you are in my way?'

Kimya was standing in one corner of the terrace, feet apart, barring Aishel from sweeping the spot where Father Chrisostom had been sitting the previous night.

'Don't touch my letters, Aishel, please don't.'

'Your letters! This scribble in the dust! Why don't you help me to clean up instead of making such a fuss?'

'Father Chrisostom wrote them himself to show me. Please, Aishel, please.'

Aishel shook her head, exasperated. 'You're mad, Kimya! All this writing is nonsense. What do you need it for? Will writing help you to make bread or milk the goats?'

Kimya was now staring at her sister in desperation. Aishel heaved a sigh. It was useless to argue. Trying to talk sense with Kimya was like facing a wall. It was always the same; in the end, Kimya would either cry or she would smile to herself and forget the

دوست

rest of the world and its inhabitants. How irritating!

'You're driving us all mad, Kimya,' Aishel exclaimed.

Kimya's lips began to tremble, her eyes welling up into tears, which started to run down her cheeks. 'I can't explain, I can't explain,' she stammered, her hand on her lips, as if trying to hold back a sob. 'I want to learn how to read. It's, it's so huge in my heart.'

'What's so huge?' Aishel asked, moved in spite of herself.

Kimya was shaking her head helplessly. 'I can't explain,' she repeated, 'I can't.'

Aishel gave up and dropped her bundle of reeds. 'Let's go and get the meal ready.'

On the terrace Evdokia had already laid out a piece of cloth in front of Farokh who had just come up and was sitting with his back against the wall. She set down the frame that was to support the large, round copper tray Aishel was bringing. On it were the usual dishes of yoghurt, honey and olives and on the side were the beakers for the tea. Behind her Kimya was carrying the terracotta dish that contained the large sheets of unleavened bread Evdokia had baked a week earlier in the communal oven. Aishel went back to the house to fetch a jug of hot tea and soon they were all eating their morning meal.

'Aishel, can you fill my beaker again? And, Kimya, please, stop dreaming and eat.' Evdokia was shaking her head in disapproval, though she was also the picture of a satisfied mother.

Like a hen surrounded by her chicks, Farokh thought, the image bringing an involuntary smile to his face.

'I'm glad to see your mood is improving,' Evdokia said ironically. 'I don't know what came over you last night, but I have not seen you looking as grim since the time of the rotten wheat.' That was how the village called that summer several years earlier, when the rain had ruined the crops, and for weeks Farokh had walked around shaking his head in despair.

The smile on Farokh's face had disappeared. 'Yes,' he said, 'I feel just about as bad.' He didn't say more, and Evdokia didn't press him. They finished their meal in silence. Aishel disappeared. Except for Kimya, who was carefully clearing the sunflower shells from the dust in the corner, Evdokia and Farokh were alone.

'I couldn't sleep last night,' Farokh muttered. Father Chrisostom's words were still echoing in his ears. 'Do you know what he suggested?' he suddenly burst out. 'Do you know what nonsense he has in mind?'

'Who? What nonsense? Tahir is still a child, he —'

'I'm not talking about Tahir.' Farokh shrugged angrily. 'I'm talking about Father Chrisostom.'

'Father Chrisostom! You must be out of your mind. Have you had a nightmare?'

'Well, in a sense, this is not far from a nightmare,' Farokh replied. 'It was last night, we were talking about ...' – Farokh made a sign with his chin towards Kimya – 'about her,' he went on, lowering his voice. 'Father Chrisostom said ...' Farokh stopped, the words choking in his throat.

'What did he say? Go on. You're making me nervous.'

'He said that she should go to Konya.' Farokh paused, then added reluctantly, 'In order to study. What do you make of that? To Konya! To study!' His voice shook with indignation.

'Shush, you're going to make yourself ill. She's not going to

دوست

Konya right now, is she?' Evdokia was talking calmly, in the same way she talked a child to sleep by telling him that, no, he was not going to bed while gently lying him down.

Farokh looked at his wife, desperate for more words of reassurance.

'Don't worry,' she said, forcing a smile. 'We don't have to think about it now.' She stood up. 'Kimya, come on, let's go to the patch. The beans need picking. Where is your sister?'

As she went to the door, she turned back and repeated, 'Don't worry. Father Chrisostom won't be back before the autumn, and in the meantime God will show us what to do.'

Farokh would never admit it aloud, but it was true that whenever he felt lost or upset, Evdokia always found a way of calming him. The weight in his stomach had lifted. Yes, after all, Father Chrisostom was not going to be back before the autumn. So many things could happen in the meantime. I'm going to check the vines, he decided. The grapes will soon be ripe.

The sun was now high. Evdokia brushed the perspiration from her forehead. She was standing between two rows of beans with Aishel and Kimya on either side. The bags had grown heavy with the onions and the beans they had picked. 'Let's stop,' she said. 'That's enough for now.'

The two girls ran out and sat on the edge of the ditch that bordered the path leading to the orchard. Aishel picked a sunflower and started to pull the seeds, which she let drop into the folds of Kimya's kaftan. Evdokia joined them and sat down heavily beside her two daughters. She was still thinking of her conversation with Farokh, wondering: Was Father Chrisostom right? Should Kimya go to Konya? It was difficult to imagine Kimya leaving the village. And yet ... perhaps this was the answer to their worries. Evdokia knew how fond the priest was of Kimya, and she trusted his wisdom. But until today she had never thought of that writing in the dust as anything other than a game. Now she could see there was more to it than she had thought. She looked at Kimya and her sister. So different from each other! She reflected that it had been more than five moons since Kimya had been forbidden to go walking on her own. She doesn't seem to mind. Strange how she still escapes us! It could well be that Kimya wouldn't mind going to Konya either. Is this what God wants? Evdokia's eyes fell on the bags full of beans and onions beside her and her thoughts moved to Ahmed in his cave. He would certainly like some vegetables, and also some fruit.

'The apricots must be ripe,' she said, standing up and stretching, her hands on her hips. Her back was aching. 'Let's go and pick a few, and together you two can take a basket to Ahmed.' She looked Kimya in the eyes, her hand on the child's shoulder. 'I'm letting you go with your sister, but no extra walks, you understand. I don't want your father to get angry with me for letting you wander around.'

Kimya jumped to her feet and there was a scream.

'Kimya, couldn't you pay attention!'

Kimya was staring at the sunflower seeds scattered at her feet. 'I forgot,' she said, more surprised than concerned.

'Can't she ever pay attention?'

'Aishel, don't fuss. It's only a few sunflower seeds. Think of the apricots instead.'

They started to walk down towards the orchard, the stream bubbling beside them. Kimya was running ahead.

دوست

He was sitting on the smooth stone at the entrance of the cave, warming himself in the afternoon sun, and didn't move when the two girls emerged from the woods. Aishel had stopped and dropped her basket. Everybody knew that Ahmed didn't care for company and would rather flee and hide than have an encounter with anyone. Yet here he was, looking as if he had been expecting them. Kimya was already in front of him with her basket full of apricots and onions.

Ahmed smiled. 'You're Kimya,' he said. 'I wondered when I would see you again.' And turning towards Aishel, he added, 'And you are her elder sister. I can see you look quite alike.'

Aishel was still standing a few steps away, looking ready to take flight.

'You mustn't be afraid,' Ahmed said. 'Today is a holiday, a holy day,' he repeated, separating the words as if that explained his breaking his rule of silence and solitude. 'Today,' he went on, 'is the day when I heard his words, exactly three moons ago.'

Kimya was already sitting on the large stone beside Ahmed, swinging her legs. Aishel cautiously came nearer.

'Who was it you heard?' Kimya asked.

Ahmed had shut his eyes, the smile on his face now gone. 'It was Maulana, Our Master,' he said slowly.

'Who is he?'

'Kimya, shush,' Aishel interjected.

But Ahmed didn't mind being asked. On the contrary! The melody he was listening to was faint perhaps, but today he wanted to share it with these two village girls. 'He is a man of wisdom,' Ahmed said. 'He is a man of God, and his words have power.' His

50

eyes now opened, Ahmed started to laugh. 'Look at me, I was an empty jug, full of wind, and now ...' His words trailed away.

'And now?' Kimya wanted to know.

'Now I am emptier than ever, but this emptiness has become a promise.'

Kimya remained silent for a while. 'What did he say?' she finally asked. 'What did Maulana say?'

'He said that everything and everyone loves the Creator and that we are always under His protection.'

'That's true,' Kimya exclaimed, 'and to Him all things shall return.'

Ahmed stood up, startled. 'What did you say? Can you repeat what you just said?'

Kimya didn't seem to understand.

Aishel intervened. 'Don't pay attention. Kimya doesn't always know what she says, or even where she is.'

But Ahmed was not listening. He was staring at Kimya. 'Please, Kimya, can you repeat what you just said?' He talked softly as one talks to a frightened animal.

'I don't know, I don't know.' She was close to tears. 'I just know that ...' She hesitated.

'What?'

'That I'm waiting for ...' Once again she stopped. 'For ...' Then she shook her head, helpless. 'I don't know.' And then, as if nothing had happened, she jumped to her feet. 'We've brought you fruit and bread and cheese, and olives and ...' She stopped. 'Can I show you my letters?' With a stick, she drew the Greek letters she had learned from Father Chrisostom.

دوست

'So you know how to write!' Ahmed was surprised. Few villagers knew how to write and read, girls even less. He was still puzzled by her repeating Maulana's words. Of course they were words from the holy Qoran, but there were many words in the Qoran. How did she know to choose these words in particular? 'Would you like to learn other letters?'

Kimya looked at him. 'You can teach me?' Her eyes were bright with excitement.

Aishel was becoming impatient. 'We must go back,' she said.

'Yes,' Ahmed said, 'yes, you must go now.'

Kimya didn't move. 'You can teach me?' she asked again.

'I can,' he said. 'Next time I'll show you some words.' He emptied the baskets into a large cloth bag. 'May God bless your family and your village.' He watched the two girls setting off and, turning back, disappeared into the cave.

And so it went. Evdokia agreed that each week Kimya would take a basket of fruit and vegetables to Ahmed, and that she could spend some time with him and learn how to write.

'If this makes you happy, why not?'

Farokh had grumbled but finally relented. 'This way,' he said, 'she won't have to go anywhere else to study.'

Sometimes Aishel accompanied Kimya. She sat, crocheting endless ribbons of white lace while Ahmed and Kimya, bent over the ground and armed with small sticks, traced strange angular signs on the earth. One day Ahmed drew a series of small curved lines instead.

'Oh, that's beautiful,' Kimya exclaimed. 'What is it?'

دوست

'This is Persian,' Ahmed replied, 'the language that is used at court by the Sultan and also by Maulana.'

'Do you speak Persian?'

'I do. It was my mother's tongue; her parents came from the East.'

Kimya kept silent for a while.

'How many languages do people speak in Konya?' she asked.

'Well, there is Greek as we speak now, and Persian, but also Arabic' – he paused – 'and more recently the language of the Turkomans, and sometimes you hear languages from further west: Venetian, Saxon, Frank.'

Kimya wondered aloud: 'Why do people speak so many languages?'

'Sometimes I, too, wonder,' Ahmed admitted, then he shrugged. 'What do we know of His will?' His face softened into a smile. 'Your question reminds me of what Maulana said that day when I decided to leave Konya.'

'What did he say?'

'I don't remember his words exactly, but it was about the many roads leading to God. He said they were infinite, but that once you have arrived, everyone realises that the goal is always the same.'

'So perhaps one day everybody will speak the same language,' Kimya exclaimed. 'But then,' she added, puzzled, 'which language shall we speak?'

Ahmed looked at her, uncertain, then his face lit up. 'You know, I think we won't need to talk. By then silence will be our common language.'

دوست

'Oh, but that would be a pity!' And turning back to the strange curved letters Ahmed had drawn, she asked, 'Please, read it to me.'

'*Doost*,' Ahmed voiced. '*Doost*,' he repeated softly, shutting his eyes.

The word felt like a caress. 'What does it mean?'

'It means "the Friend", "the One I Love", "the One I Long For".'

That night Kimya found it difficult to fall asleep. There was a sadness in her heart she didn't quite understand, yet at the same time she could feel close, so close to 'that' – whatever 'that' was – that she was waiting for. '*Doost*,' she repeated to herself, and the word vibrated within her chest. '*Doost*.' It felt like an answer, but an answer to a question she knew not. Next to her Aishel turned and moaned in her sleep. Through the narrow window a ray of moonlight was weaving itself into patterns of white lace that soon became a path climbing steeply to the sky. She began to walk up the white path. It took her beyond the village, then beyond the mountains. In the far distance, emerging from the dark, were the outlines of domes, cupolas and minarets. They began to swirl, then they turned into the folds and curves of the Persian word. '*Doost*,' she murmured as she felt herself falling into a deep softness.

'Why is everybody so late this morning?' Evdokia's voice on the other side of the wall had awakened her. 'Aishel, bring the tea on to the terrace. And where is your sister?'

Kimya stretched, feeling strangely happy. Through the window the sunlight was flooding the room. Perhaps if she closed her eyes

دوست

long enough, she could remember whom it was she had been walking with.

'Kimya, could you move?' Aishel's irritated voice startled her out of her pursuit.

'*Doost*,' she whispered to herself, '*doost*,' and she jumped out of bed.

## VIII

'TELL ME ABOUT MAULANA. DID YOU TALK TO HIM?'
Holding her knees in her hands, her brown kaftan covering
her feet, Kimya was facing Ahmed, who sat on the large flat stone
he had come to consider his own. It was grey and polished by the
elements, with a soft curve that made it especially comfortable to sit
on. He had found it one day at the edge of the forest and carried it
all the way to his cave. A perfect seat for one wanting to live simply,
he had thought at the time.

Between the two of them, drawn in the dust, the Greek letters
looked like the marks of birds' feet. Kimya was waiting for his
answer.

'I never talked to Maulana,' Ahmed said. 'You know, I only
saw him once.'

'Only once! But you said he told you—'

'I said I heard him talking,' Ahmed corrected. 'He was in his
*madrassa* speaking to a huge crowd and ...' He paused, then added,
'It was as if he had talked to me personally.'

She nodded. 'What is a *madrassa*?'

'It's a college, a place where teachers talk to the people so that
they can learn.'

'Did he wear his blue robe and his grey turban?'

Ahmed gasped. This child never ceased to amaze him. That day

دوست

in Konya when he listened to Maulana at the *madrassa*, Maulana was wearing a blue Arab robe buttoned from neck to toe, and indeed he had a grey turban on his head.

'How do you know?' he asked.

'I saw a man last night; he was wearing a blue robe and a grey turban. He had green-blue eyes. He smiled at me and took my hand.'

They remained silent.

'You're very lucky,' Ahmed said after a while. 'Perhaps one day you will meet him. Who knows?'

She was looking at Ahmed with that same seriousness that had struck him the first time he had met her and her mother near the fountain in the village.

'Yes, I will meet him.'

He was struck by the calm certainty with which she said it.

That morning when she opened the door, Evdokia sensed a new sharpness in the air. For the first time in weeks the sun had not yet reached the top of the eastern peaks.

Father Chrisostom will soon be with us, she thought. Autumn is approaching.

She gathered a few sticks from the bundle of wood heaped by the side of the house and went back in to prepare the first meal of the day. The thought of the old priest had reawakened her worries about Kimya. Those lessons with Ahmed had been a good thing. Kimya had not strayed once and Farokh had relaxed. But the child was even more estranged from her friends, and she still slipped into those absences that frightened Evdokia. Sometimes they lasted only a few seconds, but at other times it was as if the child were no longer there, her body just a shell.

Later in the afternoon, as they were slicing onions together on the roof terrace bathed in the red-gold light of the afternoon sun, Evdokia ventured: 'What happens? Where do you go in your mind in those times when you seem so far away from us all?' Almost immediately she regretted having asked. In the peacefulness of the moment the question sounded intrusive.

But Kimya didn't seem to mind. 'I don't know,' she said, putting aside her small knife and staring into the distance towards the mountains. 'I'm nowhere when it happens. I mean, I'm not here, but I'm not anywhere else either.' She frowned with the effort to make sense of her experiences. 'I feel I've arrived and I'm ... It's the same as in the dream! I'm happy and nothing is missing.'

'The dream!' Like most of her friends, Evdokia believed that God at times sent dreams to people in order to guide them. Perhaps Kimya's dream was one of those. 'What dream? Tell me.'

'The dream when I met Maulana.'

It was as if Kimya were talking of an old acquaintance, but Maulana only meant 'Our Master'. 'Who is he?' Evdokia asked, intrigued.

'Ahmed went to see him in Konya.' Kimya's eyes were bright with intensity.

In Konya! Anxiety gripped Evdokia again. Then she let out a cry. 'Look what you've made me do! I've cut my finger. It's all very good this dreaming, but it won't give us a meal.'

Kimya didn't reply. Evdokia was furious with herself. She had missed an opportunity and it was partly her fault. The child had now retreated out of reach into her usual, quiet indifference. They finished their task in silence, wiping their eyes, assailed by the acrid smell of the onions.

The first rain came, and down near the stream the poplars turned yellow. Evdokia was sitting on the stone bench outside their house, washing a batch of squashes, the last of the season. From time to time she chased away with a shush the more daring hens which were always on the lookout for extra food. She had kept her conversation with Kimya to herself. No need to make Farokh worry even more. But she wondered about this man, this Maulana. And should she let Kimya still go and spend time with Ahmed? He's feeding her with stories that are no good for her. As if she needed more dreams to fill her head! Her thoughts turned to Father Chrisostom. He should be back by now. I wonder what keeps him?

The news reached them a few days later. It must have been about noon; outside the shadows had shortened. She was coming back from picking a few turnips with Kimya when she caught a glimpse of Kave walking up the track to their house. The boy lived in a village two hours' walk from them. He and Tahir were friends and often went hunting together. What could bring him here? Kave stopped when he saw them, and after the first salutations, instead of running away as he usually did, he awkwardly rubbed his hands against his kaftan and stared down at his feet.

Suddenly apprehensive, Evdokia pressed him. 'What is it? Are you bringing us bad news?'

The boy nodded. The old priest had been found a few days earlier lying unconscious on a path leading to Kave's village. It was

دوست

Kave's mother and sister who had discovered him. 'My mother told us,' Kave said, 'that as she put her ear against Father's chest, she found that his heart was beating very fast. His breath was coming haltingly but when she poured water on his face, Father opened his eyes.' Kave remained silent, unsure of how to continue.

'What happened then?' Evdokia urged.

'Well, my sister ran back and called for help. I came with Barham and Hassan, our neighbour's sons. They're older than me and stronger,' Kave reflected aloud, 'and together we carried Father to our house.'

Apparently the priest had been given some herb potion and Kave's mother had spent the night by his side. 'But in the morning,' Kave said, 'Father Chrisostom had stopped breathing.'

Evdokia was listening, a lump in her throat. She stared at her hands, the very hands Father Chrisostom had joined with Farokh's that day in the church, some twenty years ago. Tears were now running down her cheeks. Did Father Chrisostom suffer? she wondered.

As if answering her question the boy added, 'When I came into the room in the morning and looked at Father ...there was a smile on his face.'

In the priest's pack they had found a piece of hard bread, an old wooden crucifix, the silver goblet he used for celebrating mass, two shirts, 'And also this,' Kave said, taking out of his kaftan a crinkled piece of paper with one of its corners torn. Written on it were two lines of Greek letters.

'That evening when he was still conscious, he asked my mother to fetch this from his bag and twice he said, 'For Kimya, for Kimya.'

دوست

Then, my mother says, he shut his eyes and never spoke again.'

They had been walking slowly while talking and were now in front of the house. 'What,' Evdokia asked, 'did you do for the funeral?'

'Our imam led the prayer, and we sang Christian hymns. We buried him near the church.'

Evdokia shook her head. Not even a Christian priest to attend his funeral, she thought, and again tears welled up in her eyes. But this is the way things are going nowadays. Father knew that nobody would replace him and that, one day, the church would be abandoned. Even she, in her prayers, confused Jesus with Mohammed. Of course she still went to talk to the Virgin, but like most of the women and their men in the village, she also attended the Friday prayer in their newly erected mosque. The past and the new are like the coloured threads of wool in my weaving, Evdokia thought. Would a pattern emerge in the end?

She came back to herself. In front of her Kave was biting his lips, uncertain as to what to do next. She wiped the tears from her face and, pulling her scarf over her hair, nudged Kave towards the door. 'Come in and have something to eat. You must be tired from your walk.'

The room smelled of soured milk and of smoke from last night's fire. They found Tahir already sitting in a corner. He looked surprised at the sight of Kave. 'What are you doing here?' he asked. Kave didn't answer and Tahir frowned. 'Is there something wrong?' he asked, looking at his mother.

'We won't see Father Chrisostom any more,' Evdokia said, the words coming painfully.

دوست

At that moment Aishel came in with a tray bearing six small beakers for the tea. Evdokia took it from her hands, glad to have an excuse to delay the news. Tahir was about to ask her why the priest was not to be seen any more when Farokh appeared at the door. He had been repairing the roof of the stable under the terrace and a few shavings of wood were still attached to his kaftan. He looked around while Evdokia poured the tea. Nobody spoke.

'What's the matter?' Farokh asked as he sat down. 'You all look so sombre.' Then he noticed Kave. 'Oh, have you come to bring us some bad news?' He was grinning at his joke.

'Father Chrisostom has gone,' Evdokia interrupted. 'Kave has just come to tell us.'

'Gone? Gone where?' Farokh asked.

'Father Chrisostom has passed away, that's where he's gone!' The lump in her throat was making her choke and she felt the tears swelling up again. Farokh opened his mouth, then passed his fingers through his hair as he always did when faced with things he didn't grasp. Evdokia could guess what was going through his mind. His last words to his old friend had been words of anger, and now it was too late to take them back. She handed him a beaker of tea, trying to smile through her tears.

'When did it happen?' Farokh asked.

'He passed away last week,' she said. 'He is buried in Kave's village, near the church.' She showed him the piece of paper Kave had brought, and added, 'He left this for Kimya.' She turned towards Kave: 'Tell Farokh what happened.'

Farokh listened silently, then looked at Kimya who was standing in the doorway, her eyes fixed on the paper. 'Kimya, come and sit

62

دوست

down. Perhaps you can tell us what this means.'

She shook her head. 'I already looked,' she said. 'Some of the letters I have never seen. And some are repeated several times. I don't know what it means.'

'Never mind!' Farokh said. He looked at his wife, ashamed and relieved. She knew what he was thinking, the same as she did: Now she won't have to go to Konya.

## IX

EVERY YEAR BROUGHT THE SAME MIRACLE. THE APPLES IN THE orchard swelled into full-sized fruits and turned red almost from one day to the next.

'Tomorrow we will go and pick the apples,' Evdokia announced, a few evenings after Kave's visit. Harvesting the apples marked the end of summer. It was one of the high points of the year for the children and, like the rest of them, Kimya looked forward to it.

The orchard extended along the stream, down the patchwork of gardens where the village grew its vegetables. Both orchard and gardens were protected from the wind by the same row of poplars that marked the limits of the village until one reached the forest. The orchard consisted mainly of apple trees with only a few plums and apricots, those strong enough to survive the extremes of the mountainous climate. 'Those trees are like us,' Evdokia had remarked once. 'They are strong and sturdy. They know how to endure.' In the spring the blossoms mingled in a symphony of white and pink.

That morning large cotton sheets had been spread under the trees, turning the orchard into a field of bright colours. The children climbed into the trees and started to pick the fruit, which they dropped into the baskets held up by the women. Everybody chatted and laughed while the younger children ran around catching the apples that missed the baskets. Kimya was not sure which she pre-

دوست

ferred, picking the apples in the trees, or catching them on the ground. It didn't matter much to her. What she liked most was the smell, which suffused the village for days on end as most of the fruit was taken to be stored, while some was eaten stewed or mashed, or cut into fine slices and hung on strings to dry in sweet-scented garlands.

'Kimya, Aishel, tomorrow you will take some apples to Ahmed,' Evdokia said that same evening. They were all sitting on the terrace, tired and content. The night was clear and still warm for the season. 'I'm sure he has never eaten apples like ours in Konya,' she added.

'And I will take Father Chrisostom's paper,' Kimya said. 'Ahmed will tell me about the letters I don't know.'

Farokh shook his head in disapproval, but before he could say a word, Evdokia stopped him with a frown. 'Let it be,' her eyes were saying. 'It's only a piece of paper.'

'The letters might mean something,' Kimya said. 'I'm sure Father Chrisostom will help and tell us.'

Evdokia shuddered. Perhaps the old priest was not so far, after all. Farokh looked up to the stars with a sigh. The nonsense women could utter!

Kimya slowed down, letting Aishel go ahead. Her basket was heavy with the usual piece of cheese and folds of bread sheets, plus today the apples as well as some squashes and onions. She pushed back a few wisps of hair under her headscarf and stood listening. The noise from the village had vanished. Around her the silence was alive with whispers: a branch cracking nearby, the buzzing of insects, Aishel's footsteps fading away and, as always, the birds' twittering.

دوست

All this enclosed in dancing patterns of light and shadows. She shut her eyes for a second, filled with a feeling of contentment which grew into an almost unbearable joy.

'Kimya, Ki-my-a …' Aishel's voice, in the distance, sounded worried. She opened her eyes and caught sight of a squirrel busily burying a hazelnut in the ground.

'I'm coming,' she shouted and started to walk on again, feeling that she too had buried something precious in the woods. What that was, though, she had no idea.

'I wasn't expecting you so soon!' Ahmed looked surprised at seeing the two girls.

Kimya noticed he was wearing the old green tunic they had recently given him, which was now too small for Farokh.

'It's apple time,' Aishel said in explanation. 'Mother wanted you to have some.'

Kimya couldn't wait. 'I have something to show you,' she said, unfolding Father Chrisostom's piece of paper, and handing it over to Ahmed.

'Let's sit down first,' Ahmed said, clearing the ground with his hands. Having taken the piece of paper, he looked at it carefully for a while. He then raised his head. 'Where does this come from?' He looked puzzled or perhaps worried. It was difficult to tell.

'This is what Father Chrisostom left for Kimya,' Aishel explained. 'He said this was for her.' She paused. 'He said this just before he died.'

'And you don't know what it means?'

Kimya shook her head. 'It's not like the letters he gave me to copy.'

دوست

'No, of course, it's a message … addressed to you, Kimya.'

Addressed to her! She remembered the spark in Father Chrisostom's eyes when they talked together, and also his tired smile the last time he had visited the village.

Ahmed passed his fingers through his beard. 'Kimya, do you have any idea what Father Chrisostom is saying in his message?'

She shook her head again. 'I don't know. I think he wants me to learn more.'

'That is true,' Ahmed said. 'He wants you to study, and for that he wants you to go to Konya.'

The two girls were speechless. Ahmed, too, looked astonished at the message from the old priest.

'Is that all?' Kimya asked after a while.

Ahmed unfolded the paper once again. 'No, not quite. He says Sister Andrea of the Convent of St Peter will help you.'

Konya! Sister Andrea! The Convent of St Peter! The words were spinning in Kimya's head. 'But I don't want to go to Konya!' she exclaimed. She could not quite imagine a life away from the village. What was a city like? Was there a forest nearby where one could go and hide? Were there streams to cool oneself in the summer? And what about Baba and her mother! How could she leave them? Suddenly short of breath she looked at Ahmed in a panic.

'Don't you want to go to Konya?' Ahmed asked.

The tone of his voice startled her. She remembered the domes and the minarets of her dream, the man in his blue robe holding her hand, and more than anything the joy and sense of belonging she had then felt.

'Don't you know?' Ahmed said quietly. 'Don't you know that

دوست

there is something waiting for you in Konya? This something has to do with Maulana; of that I'm certain.' He paused for a while. His face had softened. 'You mustn't be afraid,' he added gently. 'Everything will happen as it must.'

Ahmed's words were soothing. He was looking deep into her eyes. Her fear receded, replaced by a great calm which she felt enfolded the three of them. Perhaps there was nothing to decide, after all. Life carried you along and you just went with it.

'Kimya, you must tell your parents.' Ahmed's voice was serious. They remained silent for a while until Ahmed shook himself out of his thoughts. 'Let me show you the letters you don't know and how they make words.'

This time Aishel, too, bent over the strange signs Ahmed was drawing on the ground. So that was what writing did! It allowed someone to talk to you, even after he had died! She looked at her sister who was now repeating the sound of each letter after Ahmed, her usual irritation at Kimya turning into sadness.

'Oh, Kimya, you won't go to Konya?'

Ahmed looked up. Aishel was crying and he put his hand on her arm. 'Sometimes God wants things we think we don't want,' he said.

Angrily she pushed him away.

Kimya was gazing at her hands. What did God want? Did He really want her to go to Konya? A sudden burst of wind rustled the pines around them.

'Let's pray,' Ahmed said, and he started to recite: *'Bismillah ir rahman ir rahim* – In the name of Allah, most gracious and most merciful ...' The girls knew the prayer. These were the words the imam recited when starting the Friday prayer. They held their

دوست

hands open to receive the grace, then they all prostrated themselves. '*La illa ha il Allah* – God is the only Reality.' They washed their faces with the grace that now filled their hands. The prayer was over and Ahmed proceeded to empty the baskets.

'You must go back and tell your parents,' he said again.

Aishel looked at him sternly. 'Baba won't let her go,' she said. 'He won't.' There was fear as well as stubbornness in her voice.

'Perhaps not yet,' Ahmed said. 'God knows what is best. Nothing is of our own doing.'

'Kimya is not going to Konya! She is not.' Farokh was pacing back and forth, his face flushed with rage, his fists clenched.

Gathered around the evening meal, the family kept silent while darkness slowly engulfed the room as the sun outside sank behind the mountains.

Evdokia broke the silence. 'We'll talk with the imam; he was Father's friend and—'

'I'm not going to talk to anyone,' Farokh interrupted. 'I'm not.' His whole being was screaming NO.

Evdokia looked at her husband with a sigh. 'Sit down, Farokh, you're making me dizzy.'

Farokh stopped pacing and looked at his wife, weighing in his mind whether sitting down was the beginning of a dangerous concession. He decided that possibly it was not and sat down between his son and his wife.

'How could he do that?' he asked. He was apparently talking to himself, and no one ventured an answer. 'This is treacherous,' he continued, this time addressing his wife.

دوست

Evdokia calmly tore some bread, folded it and wiped up the rest of the beans at the bottom of the dish. She nodded towards the tray. 'Kimya, Aishel, clear up and go and milk the cow,' she ordered. 'And Tahir, you go and collect fodder for the goats.' She waited until the three of them had left.

'There,' she said, 'now we can talk.' She smoothed the cushion between them. 'What do you mean, treacherous?' she asked.

Farokh was drinking his tea, a stubborn frown on his face. 'Leaving a message like this! His last will!' He sniffed in disgust. 'He's dead,' he said angrily. 'How can we argue with him? How much more treacherous can one be? And now that she knows, it will go to her head ...'

'Shush, it had to come out into the open,' said Evdokia. 'Since Father told you in the summer, we have both been thinking about it. Well, now it's in the open, perhaps it's better that way.'

Farokh scratched his head. Yes, it was now public knowledge. The women would talk with their men who would each have something to say for or against Kimya's departure, and each would feel entitled to give advice. He sighed; the weight in his chest was too heavy to bear.

Evdokia put her hand on his arm. 'Kimya said that Father Chrisostom left the name of a Christian nun, a Sister Andrea who could take care of her in Konya.'

Farokh didn't seem to hear, then suddenly he covered his face with his hands and his shoulders started to shake with uncontrollable sobs. 'I can't let her go,' he muttered. 'I can't. She is my light ...' He was now groaning, his whole body shaking as if swept by a storm.

دوست

Never had Evdokia seen her husband in such a state, not even at the time when the rain had ruined the crops. She waited. The braying of a donkey in the distance brought them back to the present. Farokh's sobs were subsiding. He uncovered his face and looked helplessly at Evdokia, tears still streaming down his cheeks. She, too, began to cry. Farokh doesn't know it yet, she thought, but in spite of himself, he has come to a decision. Kimya would go and study in Konya.

'Farokh' – Evdokia stroked her husband's hand – 'you know she can always come back.'

He shook his head. He was gazing at the carpet. 'She won't come back if she leaves. She doesn't belong here.'

So, he had finally voiced what they both feared and knew, without ever having admitted it to each other! The room was now dark with only the red glow of the embers in the hearth. 'We've always known it,' she said softly, 'haven't we?'

He nodded, unable to talk, his face still wet with tears. They remained lost in their thoughts until Evdokia heard the sound of the door.

'It's cold outside.' It was Aishel carrying a bundle of dry twigs. She put it down beside the fireplace and rubbed her hands. Bending down, she started to revive the fire.

'Winter will soon be with us,' Evdokia said and, as always with the coming of winter, she thought of the traveller of eight years ago. He had been right: the baby she was then carrying had been a girl, and they had indeed obeyed him and called her Kimya. What had happened to him? she wondered. In the hearth the flames licked the walls. She turned towards Farokh. 'Kimya can go in the spring,'

71

دوست

she said. 'There's no hurry.'

Farokh didn't reply.

The news had spread rapidly through the village. Since Ahmed's arrival some six months ago, nothing very exciting had happened, and Kimya going to study in Konya because of something Father Chrisostom had scribbled on a piece of paper – this was news. Aishel had told her best friend, Muesser, who had told her mother, who had told her husband. And Evdokia had confided in Maria, her old friend from childhood, herself a mother of five.

'What are we to do?' Evdokia asked. The two women were washing clothes a short distance away from the fountain, enfolded as usual in clouds of steam. 'You know Kimya has her own ways,' she continued, 'but since Ahmed has been teaching her, she hasn't strayed once as she used to.' Evdokia was almost talking to herself. 'She does like to study, there's no doubt about it. But Farokh is so upset ...'

Maria sat up and wiped her hands on her kaftan. 'Father Chrisostom was a wise man,' she said. 'You must trust him ... and trust in God,' she added.

Evdokia brushed a wisp of hair out of her eyes and started to beat the pile of clothes in front of her angrily. Maria was a good woman, but she was not sending any of her own children away.

Not everyone agreed that Kimya should go.

'I wouldn't let Kimya go to Konya, if she were mine,' Safia said to her mother. She was stirring a pot of steaming soup while pushing one of her breasts between the lips of her latest child, a boy who kept

72

دوست

refusing it, and then cried in frustration. 'What would I do in my old age?' she continued. 'We need all the help we can get when we're old.'

'That's true,' Usha, her mother, agreed. 'What will she do with all her studies?' The old woman sniffed disapprovingly. 'No man will ever want to marry her. Too much brain in a woman doesn't do her any good.'

'What does the imam say?' Safia's husband had just entered the room and found himself pulled into the discussion.

'He says that Father Chrisostom might be right and that people should stop talking so much and pray instead,' Safia answered.

'Well, he should know that as far as you women are concerned, silence is not what you're best at.'

Safia laughed and handed him the baby, who was still crying. 'Kimya is a strange child, that's all I can say. I'm glad my children are just like any other children.'

## X

WINTER HAD COME ALL OF A SUDDEN. THE PREVIOUS evening they were still sitting on the roof terrace sipping tea around the fire, but this morning a fine layer of snow was covering the village and the surrounding slopes.

'It's only November,' Evdokia complained. 'What about my beans and my squashes?'

Farokh, too, was worried about the frost. 'I must go and have a look at the vines; I haven't finished pruning them yet.' I should have started earlier, he grumbled to himself. I've waited too long this year. He gulped his tea down and rushed towards the door. 'Tahir, come on, we've got work to do.'

'You're not going like that, without your coat, are you?' Evdokia cried.

He shrugged and was already on his way when she came to the door with his felt coat. She stood in the doorway watching the dark shapes of Farokh and Tahir disappearing in the snow, already blurred by the mist.

'He thinks he's still young,' she muttered to herself as she re-entered the house. She hung up the coat and pulled her shawl around her shoulders. 'It's cold,' she said aloud, as if she could not believe it. Her mind went back to the vegetable patch.

'Aishel, Kimya, let's go and pick the beans and the squashes

دوست

before they are wasted.'

It was early afternoon when Farokh and Tahir came back.

'You've had nothing to eat since last night,' Evdokia reproached them. 'This is not good.' Farokh looked exhausted. She noticed his pinched nostrils and how the blood had drained from his face. His skin seemed more the colour of bone than flesh.

He collapsed on the cushions and wiped his forehead. 'I think we were just in time,' he said.

The grapes were one of their few sources of income and they could not afford to lose the harvest. Every year at the end of summer the young men of the villages carried down baskets full of grapes to the nearest cities of Laranda and Konya. They started at dawn and went from village to village collecting the youths and their grapes until they all joined in a dusty turmoil of mules and donkeys. And every year it was the same: 'Tahir, what will you bring me back?' Aishel asked.

'And me, and me?' Kimya sang. 'Will you bring me a bracelet?'

'Don't forget to buy a knife,' Evdokia would say. 'Ours is broken; and if you find a good, strong, ewer—'

'Enough, enough,' Tahir cried. 'What if I don't sell my grapes?'

'If you don't sell your grapes,' Farokh said with a grin, 'you'd better not show your face here again.' They both knew there was no risk of Tahir not selling his grapes. True, most people in the cities grew their own fruit and vegetables, but there were also many travellers and many newcomers there who didn't have their own piece of land, and the grapes grown on the slopes of the villages were always in demand.

دوست

But today the grapes and their sale were far from Evdokia's thoughts. She looked at her husband, concerned. Prostrate against the cushions, he was shivering.

'You stubborn old fool,' she said, her irritation turning to worry. She went out of the room and came back carrying a thick blanket in one hand and a bowl of hot soup in the other. 'Get yourself near the fire,' she grumbled, wrapping the blanket around Farokh's shoulders. 'And eat this,' she added as she handed him the bowl of soup. 'Tahir, go and help yourself.'

She sat down beside Farokh, who ate the soup in silence. 'You're not going to be ill, are you?' she asked, mostly to reassure herself.

He soon handed her the empty bowl and shut his eyes. 'I'll be all right, don't you worry. I'll be all right,' he repeated, adding involuntarily, 'I'm so tired.' A few minutes later, he was asleep.

The next morning he was hot and agitated, and stayed in bed. Evdokia and Aishel took turns by his side laying cold compresses on his forehead, but at the end of the day he was delirious, muttering words Evdokia could not catch. Early the next morning, she decided to go and ask for help from old Serena.

Old Serena lived alone on the edge of the village, the only survivor of an attack by a group of passing soldiers which several years earlier had wiped out all the people of the village where she had been born and married, including her husband and four children. The day the soldiers had arrived, just after dawn, she was roaming the hills on one of her quests for medicinal plants. She had heard the cries and seen the smoke rising in the distance, but when she returned home all she found was an eerie silence hovering over smouldering

دوست

ruins stained with blood. Serena had found refuge in Evdokia's village which, thanks to its remoteness, had been spared the passage of troops and invaders through the years. She had been given a house, more of a one-room hut, and the villagers had shared their food with her until she was able to grow her own and keep a few chickens. She spent most of her time picking plants and herbs in the mountains and making bitter potions which, she said, could cure most of the ailments the villagers suffered from. She never talked about her past and the villagers were mixed in their feelings towards her. The strange invocations she whispered when preparing and administering her potions and ointments frightened them, and they came to her only when desperate for help. The imam had been heard grumbling that if only people had faith and if only they prayed, they wouldn't have to go and ask an old witch for healing.

'There is only God to invoke,' he said, angry at the way people slipped back to the ancient pagan practices. And Evdokia had also heard Father Chrisostom remark that the calling of spirits to bring cures and make women fertile was no more than superstition. 'The old beliefs of pagan times are only doors through which the devil can enter,' he would often say. Serena, it was true, went neither to the mosque nor the church. She was definitely an outsider in spite of having lived in the village for many years now. Yet regardless of their fears, Evdokia and most of her friends couldn't help thinking that the more help one can get, the better. If God is loving and compassionate, as both the priest and the imam say He is – well, certainly He doesn't mind people trying to get additional help from kind spirits, whoever they are.

Outside, a chilly drizzle made her walk faster and wrap her

shawl closer around her. When she pushed open the door of Serena's lodging, there was Serena bent over a mortar, busy crushing seeds. The space around her was filled with pots and jugs of all sizes and shapes. On the fire a thick, dark mixture was simmering, filling the air with a pungent smell.

'Let me finish this,' Serena said, without turning to look at her visitor.

She was wearing a kaftan of an undefined colour, half brown, half grey, which was fringed at the hem. Her headscarf had slipped, revealing wisps of grey, matted, curly hair. Evdokia sat down on a small stool and waited. She couldn't help feeling apprehensive. Serena is not a bad woman, she told herself. Sometimes she does help.

'There,' Serena said. She put down the small mortar and, wiping her hands on a piece of cloth, turned towards Evdokia. 'Oh, it's you!' she exclaimed. 'How is the family? Your girls, and your beautiful boy? Nothing wrong with them, I hope?' She was unusually welcoming.

'No,' Evdokia said, 'no, God be praised, they are all in good health.'

'Woman's change of age?' Serena ventured.

'No, no,' Evdokia said again. 'It's Farokh. I'm so worried.'

Serena's eyes narrowed. 'What is the matter? A fall?'

'Not a fall,' Evdokia said. 'He came back two days ago from working on the vines. He had not worn his coat. Last night he kept tossing and turning and now he's very hot and delirious, and ...' She didn't finish her sentence, but wrung her hands.

'Hmm, caught a cold,' Serena muttered to herself. She looked sternly at Evdokia. 'You're not telling me everything; he's worrying

78

about something. What is it?'

'Well, the vines not being pruned, and the cold so early—'

Serena brushed away Evdokia's words with an irritated gesture of the hand. 'Not that!' she said. 'I mean he's worried about something in the family. Isn't he?' She waited, her eyes now half closed.

Evdokia was feeling more and more uneasy. Perhaps Father Chrisostom and the imam were right, after all. Perhaps Serena was an old witch, dealing with evil and not to be trusted. I should never have come, she thought.

'Look, Evdokia,' Serena said, 'if you want me to help you, I have to know the whole story. There's no point in telling me only half of it.'

Evdokia felt like a child scolded by her mother. 'Well,' she admitted, 'Farokh is worried about Kimya ...' She paused, then she added, 'But this has nothing to do with his catching a bad cold ...'

'Tttt, tttt, perhaps, perhaps,' Serena agreed, 'but it has a lot to do with his recovering from it.'

Evdokia sat back, forced to admit that there was some truth in what Serena was saying. And it was true that since they had decided to send Kimya to study in Konya, Farokh was not as quick to get up in the morning as he used to be. His walk had lost its spring, and he kept losing his temper, especially when Kimya mentioned her lessons with Ahmed.

'All that nonsense! Will that ever help you to cook or to milk the goats?' he had burst out one evening, and then rushed out into the night, to come back only hours later.

'I've heard that Kimya is soon to go to Konya,' Serena was saying. 'And that's good, you know,' she added, to Evdokia's surprise. 'But,' Serena continued, 'Farokh has to accept her going

دوست

from the bottom of his heart.' She looked at Evdokia piercingly. 'Otherwise,' she said, 'it will kill him.'

Evdokia shivered. Serena's words were cold and sharp: like the blade of a knife, she thought. And they were going straight to the core of her anxiety about both Farokh and Kimya.

Serena brusquely took a jug from the shelves and poured a brown liquid from it into a small flask, which she handed to Evdokia. 'Give him this twice a day, it will help,' she said matter-of-factly. She paused for a second and then continued, 'But he must let her go, you understand. Love has nothing to do with keeping those you love around.' Her lips were tight and she was gazing into the distance.

Evdokia stood up, finding nothing to say.

'Love,' Serena went on, 'is that link between people which makes them blossom. But for the full blossoming to happen, the link has to be severed, always.' Her face had taken on a fierce, stony expression. 'Love's task is to take us beyond the realm of separation. It has nothing to do with happiness here.'

She talked with a certainty filled with an almost menacing power. All Evdokia wanted to do now was to get away. She put down the apples and the honey she had brought on a shelf. 'Thank you,' she said, opening the door. 'May God help us all.'

But Serena was beyond hearing.

The fresh air was a relief after the acrid and stuffy atmosphere of Serena's place. She walked home rapidly, holding the small flask in her hand. What was it Serena had said? Something about love and links having to be severed. She walked faster, trying to brush Serena's words out of her mind. The potion would help, so Serena had said. The rest, she preferred to forget.

## – XI –

'BABA, HERE'S SOME TEA FOR YOU,' SHE SAID SOFTLY, bending over the bed.

The room was dark, the window covered with a cloth. It smelled of illness. Lying under a thick brown blanket, his head supported by several cushions, Farokh seemed asleep, though Kimya had heard him coughing only a few minutes earlier. 'Shall I help you?' she said, holding the beaker of tea near his lips.

He opened his eyes and for a second he didn't seem to recognise her. Then his face lit up. 'Ah, it's you, Kimya,' he murmured. 'You are not gone yet.' He pushed the beaker away. He sounded surprised and relieved.

'I won't go before you get well,' she said firmly.

He started to cough again and she waited.

'You know,' he said, after he had recovered, 'you know I won't prevent you from going?'

'I know, Baba, but you must get better first.'

Farokh had raised his head slightly. 'It breaks my heart to let you go,' he said. There were tears in his eyes.

She stood up, alarmed. 'Baba, if your heart breaks, mine too will break; then I won't go, but …' She was trying to find the right words. 'But we mustn't let our hearts break.' She was vehement. 'It's not allowed.'

دوست

Farokh let himself fall back on his cushions. 'Kimya,' he murmured, tears now rolling down his cheeks, 'Kimya, why? Why?'

She bent down again and held the small beaker to his lips. 'Baba, you mustn't cry,' she said, wiping his face with a piece of cloth. 'I am sad too, but we mustn't let our hearts break, even if it's very hard. It's not allowed.'

He grasped her hand and stared at her. She was so pretty, so composed. A calm healing strength was emanating from her and for a moment he felt that she was much older than him. He shut his eyes again and repeated her last words. 'Not allowed. Yes,' he said, 'you're right ... but it's so hard.' Old memories were surfacing: the blizzards of winter-time spiralling into golden summer days, Evdokia's father smiling at him, the light of a candle on the face of his newborn son. 'Life,' he murmured, 'life.' The coolness of the hand on his forehead seemed to confirm that, yes, life was made of many hues, all to be lived to the full. The hand left his forehead, he heard the sound of footsteps followed by the door creaking and then all was silence. And in that silence it came to him that, however painful it might be, he would survive Kimya leaving the village. A sense of well-being he had not felt for months flooded him and he let himself fall into a deep peace which was neither happiness nor sadness, but more like balm on a wound.

It took a few more days for the fever to recede and for the coughing to stop. When he emerged from the house, a week later, still wobbly on his legs, Farokh was thinner, but the spark in his eyes was back and he walked with his old determination. It was not such a bad idea, after all, to go and ask for Serena's help, Evdokia thought. No

دوست

more mention had been made of Kimya and her going to Konya until one morning she found Farokh in front of the house checking the donkey's hooves.

'I'm making sure it can sustain the journey to Konya,' he said, before she could ask a question. She stared at him uncomprehendingly and he added, 'For Kimya's journey.'

'You mean she's going *now*?'

Farokh bent forward over the donkey's hoof, avoiding her eyes. 'Why wait any longer? Once a decision is made, it's better to act.'

Impatient, the donkey kicked and Farokh let the animal move towards a tuft of thistles a few feet away. He turned to face his wife. 'I will go with her and make sure she's in good hands,' he said.

Serena's warning was still ringing in her ears: 'Farokh has to accept Kimya going; otherwise, it will kill him.' Well, Farokh had accepted. And now he was back on his feet, and Kimya was going. There is always a price to pay, Evdokia thought. There was nothing more to say.

That evening after preparing the meal, she went to the church. It was dark except for a small candle burning on the altar she knew so well, the altar consecrated to the Virgin. Who could have lit that candle? she wondered. So few people went to the church these days! She knelt in front of the Virgin. 'Please, give me strength,' she prayed. When she stood up, she could have sworn the painting on the wall was smiling at her.

They left one morning in late November, just after dawn. Kimya was sitting on the donkey, surrounded by the bundles of food and clothes Evdokia had prepared the previous evening. Evdokia was standing at the door, tears running down her face. She suddenly turned away. 'Wait. I want to give you something.' She disappeared into the house and came back a few seconds later holding what looked like a small, carved piece of wood. She handed it to Kimya. 'This is for you, so that Mary will protect you.'

It was a set of three tiny panels of wood hinged together, the two smaller ones opening on a painting of the Virgin with her child on a background of gold. On each side of her stood two angels, and both the Virgin and Evdokia had the same look of quiet strength, filled with tenderness. Only the Virgin was not weeping; she was smiling.

'We'll be all right,' Kimya said, and Evdokia knew that she meant, 'You and I will be all right.'

She nodded to show she understood and then, looking at Farokh, she said angrily, 'What are you waiting for? Go.'

As the donkey started to move, with Farokh walking in front pulling the reins, Kimya looked back one last time. Evdokia didn't look angry at all; she was wiping the tears from her face.

Of the journey Kimya would remember the sound of the stones rolling under the donkey's hooves, the sudden flight of a bird disturbed by their passage, the landscape seemingly turning on itself, mountain range after mountain range, the light playing through the trees, constantly changing as the day wore on.

They spent their first nights with families in various villages along the way. Somewhere a woman placed a small child in her arms. For a moment she looked at the tiny face and wondered: Did babies dream of stars or angels, or simply of their mother's breast? The next day the path widened into a larger track; they left the mountains behind and entered a flat landscape where bushes and rocks gave way to cultivated fields and orchards. Here there were other donkeys trotting along beside them and rattling carts pulled by mules and horses. There were also people on foot. Soon, a few wooden houses loomed up by the side of the road.

It was late afternoon when finally the outlines of domes and minarets appeared in the distance. 'Baba, look. We are arriving.' She could hardly believe her eyes. It was the same landscape she had seen in her dream. And the same joy she had felt in the dream was now flooding her heart. This is home, she said softly to herself. How strange! Yet it was true.

Along the road the orchards were now expanding into gardens. Soon they found themselves facing the walls of the city in front of which stretched a great square, half of it covered with tents in all shades of brown. In and out of them, constantly moving, came a stream of men, women and children. In the space still free of tents young men on horses were racing in short bursts of frenzied galloping.

With hundreds of other people they entered the city through a huge, carved stone gate surmounted by a large tower. The noise was deafening, the air cloudy from the dust raised by the trampling of so many feet. In the crowd Kimya caught sight of a boy not much older than herself who was selling square pastries covered with sesame seeds.

It was years since Farokh had been in Konya, but nothing much had changed. The bazaar on the western side of the city had grown, but the narrow alleys and their lines of shops were much the same,

دوست

with the shopkeepers sitting on the doorstep as ready as ever to draw the customer in. They walked through the lanes. One smelled of leather, with nothing but shoes and bags of all sizes and colours displayed on each side; one was filled with the clatter of hammering, with goldsmiths and silversmiths bent over their anvils. Farokh kept walking. They crossed a lane lined with jewellery shops and Kimya gazed at the glittering display. But Farokh didn't stop. They passed through a lane where all sorts of fabric and cloth were exhibited in an array of colours, and finally emerged into a small square with a fountain in the middle. The square was surrounded with shops overflowing with bags of yellow, green and red powders, or with large pieces of meat hanging on hooks.

'Let's see if Hakan is here,' Farokh said, heading to one of the shops.

Hakan was sitting on the doorstep, surrounded by bags of grain. He had a small red cap on his head and, like most people in Konya, he was wearing his hair split into two long plaits. 'What a surprise!' he said with a large smile when seeing his old friend. 'What brings you here, and who is this little one?'

'This is Kimya,' Farokh said, proudly nudging Kimya in front of him.

They sat down, and glasses of *chai* appeared. They exchanged news about their families, the weather and the latest wars in the region. The Mongols were getting nearer and people were afraid.

'Hundreds of refugees are arriving every day,' Hakan said. 'You saw them camping outside the city. They say whole cities are being burned down, thousands of people massacred.' Hakan looked at Farokh with a tired smile. 'These are troubled times,' he said with

86

دوست

a sigh. 'But tell me, what brings you here with your daughter?'

Farokh took a sip of his tea, then cleared his throat. Hakan was waiting.

'I'm taking Kimya to the Convent of St Peter,' Farokh said finally. 'Do you know where it could be?'

Hakan looked surprised at the news, but made no comment. And yes, he knew of a convent nearby where young children were taught by Christian nuns. 'I am not sure, though, what the name of the convent is,' he said.

They spent the night with Hakan and his family, and the next morning left the donkey with them and went in search of the convent. On the way Farokh was told the one Hakan had mentioned was indeed the Convent of St Peter. Soon they found themselves in front of a large, carved, wooden door with a shining copper knob. Farokh hesitated. Was it really here that he would leave Kimya? He looked at her standing beside him. She was very quiet; she, too, seemed unsure. Reluctantly he knocked at the door and a small window opened in the middle of it, framing the stern face of a woman.

'What is your request?' the face asked.

'I would like to speak to Sister Andrea.' The name of this unknown sister sounded strange, almost incongruous, on his lips.

'Sister Andrea is not here any more,' said the face. 'She has gone back to Constantinople. What do you want?'

Farokh felt relieved. If Sister Andrea was not there, Kimya could not go into this convent. Could she? The face was still waiting for an answer.

'Nothing,' he finally said, 'nothing.' He turned away and as he took Kimya's hand, he heard the window slamming behind them. They wandered for a while, Farokh at a loss. What should he do now? Should he go back to the convent, after all? But the thought of having to talk with the woman behind the door again made him recoil.

They had reached a small square shaded with plane trees. From a niche carved in a wall, the cheerful sound of a fountain welcomed them. Farokh sat down on the rim and put his hand in the water. It was fresh and invigorating. He looked at Kimya. She started to play with the water, trying to catch the drops shimmering in the light. She was now singing softly to herself as if the whole journey to Konya, the search for the convent, the quest for Sister Andrea, had nothing to do with her.

Was it all a mistake? Farokh wondered. Should they go back to the village and forget the whole idea of Kimya's studying here?

A commotion at the corner of the square interrupted his thoughts. A small crowd was entering the square, surrounding a man riding a mule. The man was wearing a blue robe, and he had a grey turban on his head. From his whole being emanated a feeling of warmth and kindness, though his eyes looked sharp and alert.

Nothing can escape this man, Farokh thought. He noticed that everybody in the crowd looked at the man with great reverence.

From all the surrounding streets people were appearing, most of them running. Some clapped their hands. Children were crying out, 'Maulana, Maulana.'

At that moment Farokh caught sight of Kimya. She was standing in front of the fountain, pale and motionless, her eyes fixed on the man on his mule.

دوست

What happened next, Farokh would never forget. The man moved towards the fountain and then, once in front of Farokh and his daughter, he dismounted. His eyes, blue-green and full of sparks, met Farokh's.

'Is this your daughter?' he asked, indicating Kimya, more as an introduction than a question.

'She is my daughter,' said Farokh. 'Her name is Kimya.'

'And you are looking for a place for her to study?'

Farokh gasped. How did this man know? He nodded, unable to speak.

'What if she came to live with my family?' the man asked almost casually, as if this were the most natural thing to suggest. 'My two sons would be happy to have a sister, and my wife would be delighted to have such a daughter as yours.'

The quiet strength the man exuded was contagious and Farokh felt his fears, his doubts, his pain vanish, himself submerged by a flow of warmth.

'This child is a precious jewel,' the man continued, 'and your love for her' – his eyes were now digging deep into Farokh's – 'your love shines too, as bright as a jewel.'

Never had Farokh felt so overwhelmed. He wanted to kneel before this man, he wanted to kiss his hand; but all he did was stand there, scratching his head and trying in vain to stop the tears from running down his face. In front of him the silhouette of Maulana – for this was the name he had already given the man – was blurred. Around them the crowd had fallen silent.

Maulana put his hand on Farokh's heart. 'By accepting your daughter's destiny,' he said, 'you have brought God's blessing on yourself and your family.' He lifted his hand, then turned towards Kimya. 'Would you like to come and live with me?'

Kimya didn't seem surprised. To Farokh's amazement she asked, 'When we walked together, were you taking me to your house?'

Maulana smiled, then nodded. 'You're right. We have already walked a long way together.' Then addressing Farokh, he said, 'Come with me. You will rest with us as long as you wish, then you will go back to your village.'

And as if the whole question were now settled, he remounted his mule. 'Kimya will be happy here,' he added, as if talking to himself.

As he joined the small crowd of Maulana's followers, Farokh heard one of them murmur, 'Glory be to God.' He was feeling strangely light and joyous. 'Glory be to God,' he repeated. Beside him Kimya was laughing.

# – XII –

SHE WAS STANDING IN THE DOORWAY WATCHING FAROKH AND the old donkey walk away. It was a grey morning drowned in a fine drizzle, which turned everything to a blurred reflection. The last two days had gone very fast. The first evening Maulana's wife, Kerra, had prepared a special meal to celebrate Kimya's arrival and they had all sat round the fire in the large kitchen, eating lamb and vegetables. There was a baby asleep in a cradle tucked into a corner of the room.

'My latest son, Alim,' Maulana explained. Later on a young man had entered who was introduced as Sultan Walad, Maulana's eldest son. 'Ala ud din is staying with his friends Hassan and Akbar,' Sultan Walad said. 'He will come later.'

Who is Ala ud din? Kimya had wondered. She vaguely remembered Maulana murmuring with a sigh that there was better company than Hassan and Akbar, and that a moment later he had started to tell a story. After that she must have fallen asleep, for the next morning she found herself lying in a small room on a pile of cushions, with a sheep's fleece spread over her, and no memory of the story. Somewhere a baby was crying. She got up and retraced her steps to the kitchen where she found Kerra in front of the hearth, rocking Alim in her arms.

Kerra had welcomed her and remarked, 'Alim is only six months

91

دوست

old, but you will find him very determined.' The baby had smiled and somehow it had made her feel more at home in this new house.

Later on Farokh and she had gone back to the bazaar where Farokh had bought a woollen shawl for Evdokia. There had been more visits to friends and countless glasses of tea. She found the city and its business overwhelming. There were so many buildings and houses and people! It all seemed too big and too crowded. Then suddenly, on the previous evening around the fire in Maulana's house, Farokh had announced that he would leave in the morning.

And now his silhouette was fading away in the autumn mist. She wanted to cry out, 'Baba, Baba, do not leave,' but the lump in her throat was choking her and she couldn't utter a word, feeling suddenly lost. She was staring uncomprehendingly at two brown leaves wet from the rain at her feet when she heard someone say her name. She turned and found Kerra with Alim in her arms, a look of quiet reassurance on her face.

'You'll be all right, you'll see. Let me show you the house.' Kerra took her hand and as they went from room to room, her heart started to ease. One of the rooms overlooked a small courtyard. 'This is where you will sleep now,' Kerra said. Kimya didn't know that houses could have so many rooms nor that people could have a room all to themselves. As they passed a closed door, Kerra lowered her voice. 'This is where Maulana works,' she said.

What was Maulana's work? Kimya didn't dare ask, but Kerra was already explaining that Maulana taught at the main college every day, usually in the morning, 'And,' she said, 'sometimes also in the afternoon. And then people come and ask him for advice about their problems with their family, their business ...' Kerra's voice

دوست

trailed off and seemed suddenly tired. 'Maulana has very little time left to himself,' she added as they entered the kitchen, and Kimya wondered whether Maulana would ever have time to teach her if he were so busy.

There was something reassuring in being back in front of the large fireplace with its dark pots hung on hooks. She looked around. Stacked in the corner, the pile of clay dishes was still there, as well as the embroidered cushions in the recess of the window. At that moment a boy of about thirteen burst in. He had brown curly hair and dark eyes. He asked for water then stared at Kimya with unashamed curiosity.

'This is Ala ud din,' Kerra said, 'Ala ud din, this is Kimya. She's going to live with us.'

So this was Maulana's middle son. Kimya wondered what kept him so busy that he seemed to be hardly ever at home.

Ala ud din opened his mouth as if to say something and then, changing his mind, nodded silently and ran away.

'You mustn't pay too much attention to Ala ud din,' Kerra said. 'He's very impulsive, but he means well.'

Later Sultan Walad came in. Kimya had been too tired the other night to pay much attention to him. He was seventeen, just like her brother, but he looks older, she thought, more pensive. He had the same pale skin and the same calm gestures as Kerra, though she was only his stepmother. And while he didn't have her dark, velvety eyes, Sultan Walad had his father's eyes, blue-green and penetrating. His presence, like Kerra's, was comforting. Kerra told her a few days later that once, when Sultan Walad was only five, Maulana had taken him to the college. In front of the whole assembly the child had been asked several questions; his answers had impressed everyone with their wisdom. 'Since then,' Kerra said, 'he has attended most of his father's talks.'

As the days passed, the memory of the village began to fade, like the image of a dream, erased as it were by the tangible reality of her new life. Konya was a rich and busy city, with people coming from all corners of the world in search of fortune, knowledge, and sometimes wisdom, and she was beginning to appreciate its vibrancy. Many of the refugees who, at first, had settled on the *maidan* – the large green surrounding the city wall where the young men still rode and played polo – many of those refugees had found their way inside the ramparts as masons, carpenters and bricklayers, and through their presence the city was acquiring a whole new flavour. When going to the market, Kimya could see a group of men, not far from Maulana's house, adorning the gate of a new madrassa with fine carvings and bright turquoise ceramic tiles set in geometrical patterns, while, next to the Sultan's palace, the walls of a large mosque rose higher every day.

She enjoyed the market with its profusion of fruit and vegetables, and its commotion of people in long Arab robes, colourful kaftans and sometimes rags. One day she saw a man in strange attire – puffed sleeves and shiny velvet breeches – a Venetian merchant, she was told, whose ships were anchored in Attaleia, the city where in the winter months the Sultan had his residence. The labyrinth of the bazaar with its pungent smell of dyes, smoke and spices soon lost some of its mystery, yet none of its wonder. She found it almost as exciting as listening to Maulana's stories to walk through the narrow

دوست

alleys with the calls of the merchants, the small boys and their glasses of tea, the piles of shimmering silk, the carpets of muted colours. And she loved to listen to the ringing of hammers in the goldsmiths' lanes. Sometimes while sitting on the steps of a shop nearby waiting for Kerra, she lost herself in the rhythm of the hammering. There was also the lane of the perfume makers. She marvelled at the tiny bottles filled with scents, and shuddered at the idea of the djinn who, Maulana said, was kept captive in one of the bottles. Which one is it? she wondered. To her delight, one day a merchant rubbed a drop of scented oil the colour of amber on her wrist and the fragrance of musk stayed with her until the next morning. But still, the best part of the day was telling Maulana of her discoveries, when the whole family was assembled after the evening meal.

'What did you do today?' he would ask and she would recount the thousand and one little things that had filled her day. Maulana would listen and smile, then he would tell a story, and caravans, princesses and viziers rose from the dark, even more vivid than the whole world of the bazaar. She was the princess lying on her bed, prey to some unfathomable sorrow; she was the daughter of the woodcutter lost in the woods in search of himself; she was the King's daughter sent away into the wilderness for refusing to conform.

There were times, in the afternoon, when Maulana had visitors, and she would bring them tea or cool water flavoured with a drop of rosewater. Sometimes Maulana asked her to stay and then she would sit quietly at his feet. He and his visitors spoke mostly Persian, the language Ahmed had told her about. Now she could understand a few words here and there, sometimes a full sentence. One afternoon when she came into the study with a tray of refreshments, she found Maulana and an old friend of his sitting silent, eyes closed. The silence in the room was ringing in her ears. She felt her head spin and, placing the tray with the glasses of tea on a footstool, she quickly slipped out of the room.

'One learns to bear it,' Kerra said quietly a few minutes later when she found Kimya standing still dizzy beside the door and wondering what had happened. And for the first time Kimya noticed around Kerra's mouth two fine lines, like the imprint of a smile.

With the arrival of winter and as the cold started to bite, the family spent more time inside round the fire. Even Ala ud din seemed to abandon his friends and was now at home more often. He had taken to teasing Kimya, mocking the way she sometimes searched for a word or mispronounced it. She had learned to silence him by simply staring at him straight in the eyes with the greatest seriousness. He would then blush and leave the room grumbling about the stupidity of women.

Sultan Walad, once witnessing Ala ud din's embarrassment, had laughed. 'Not so stupid!' he said. 'Not so stupid!' And it had been Kimya's turn to feel embarrassed.

'Have the boys been teasing you again?' Maulana asked her at times. Kimya nodded, then smiled; it didn't really matter to her, and they both knew it.

In her prayers, she thanked God: 'You have given me so much! You have given me two families, and Maulana to take me to You.' And now, more meaningful, the word Ahmed had taught her came

دوست

to her lips: '*Doost*!' The Friend, the One she Longed For! A question rose in her mind. Where are You taking me? There was such sweetness in the silence that she couldn't doubt it: that sweetness was her answer.

In the orchards, a sudden burst of cloudy pink announced the end of winter. Kimya grew alarmed.

I have not been studying at all. True, her life in Konya was full and rich, but she had hardly spent any time writing as she used to do with Ahmed. Of course, she could now understand most of the words Maulana and his friends said, and she felt herself more accomplished in ways she couldn't quite define, but still, this was not study as she knew it.

That evening, she asked Maulana, 'When am I going to study?'

He looked at her, amused, then started to laugh. 'What do you think study is, little one?' he asked.

She stared at him, puzzled.

'You are studying, Kimya,' he said. 'I would even say you are one of my best students.' He remained silent for a while and Kimya felt even more puzzled. 'There are many ways to knowledge,' he continued. 'Some paths are invisible.' The tenderness in his eyes was like honey. 'Don't worry,' he said, shaking his head. 'Not seeing the path doesn't mean you're not on it; on the contrary.'

Three winters elapsed. Tahir had come several times to visit, bringing news of their parents and of the village. Everyone kept well. Safia had just had another baby boy. The grapes this year promised to be abundant. This had been her life, Kimya thought. Now it all

دوست

seemed very far away. The last time Tahir had come, she found him changed. He was now a man.

'I'm getting married,' he said, 'to Muesser, Aishel's friend.'

The imam would marry them; there would be a feast and a goat would be killed. Kimya felt a pang of nostalgia. She could almost see Aishel grumbling about her letters written in the dust, Evdokia pinning clothes on the washing line on the terrace and Baba shaking his finger at her and calling her little devil. She shook herself out of her memories. 'How is Baba?' she asked.

'He is well; he keeps himself busy. We are building a house together, the house Muesser and I will live in.'

Tahir sounded proud and happy. He didn't ask her about her life and she was relieved. Her life here was so different from the one she had had in the village! How could she tell him about it?

They stood in front of each other awkwardly until Tahir said, 'You've changed, Kimya.' He really meant: 'I don't know who you are any more.'

When he left, she had the sudden vision of a path dividing into two separate tracks, Tahir firmly walking away on one of them while she slowly set off on the other track.

'It is true, your path is a different one; but it is not for any of us to decide.'

Maulana was standing in the doorway beside her, a hint of sadness in his smile. She had not heard him coming. Together they watched Tahir disappear at the far end of the street and then, with Maulana holding her hand, they went back into the house.

A few weeks later the rumour spread. A terrible battle had taken

دوست

place somewhere in the East, in a place called Köse Dagh. The Sultan's troops had met with the Mongols and had been badly defeated.

Fear seized the city. What would happen next? Would the Mongols soon be besieging Konya? Would they sack the city and massacre its inhabitants as they had done elsewhere? A new wave of refugees made its way to the *maidan*. None of them had witnessed the event, but the mere mention of Köse Dagh brought terror into their eyes. Maulana, however, said there was nothing to fear. Konya was under God's protection and would be spared – even though, he added, 'Power is changing hands.' Then the subject was dropped. Köse Dagh was far away, after all. The new refugees pitched their tents outside the ramparts and then, as other refugees before them, they trickled into the city, and the people of Konya returned to their activities. The year was 1243 according to the Christian calendar; that is, 641 of the Hegira. Kimya had just turned eleven.

'DO YOU KNOW THE STORY ABOUT THE MOTH IN LOVE WITH the flame?'

It was late afternoon and specks of gold fluttered on the walls of the small study following the movements of the old chestnut tree in the breeze outside. Kimya had been reading a text by Attar, the great poet Maulana had met years ago when he was still a child, when Maulana had interrupted her.

'The moth,' he said, 'is so attracted by the flame that it flies nearer and nearer, until the moth is consumed.'

She didn't know the story, and she didn't think she was the moth. She was the flame, a flame at the mercy of the wind which, in Maulana's house, was blowing constantly.

Maulana had read her thoughts. 'The wind will become stronger,' he said, 'and the flame will grow, and in the end the flame, the wind and the moth will be one.'

As in answer at that moment a shiver went through the chestnut tree, scattering the fragments of gold on the walls. The love in Maulana's eyes was unbearable, and she looked away.

It was a few days later, on one of those spring mornings when everything is bathed in fresh, new light, that Maulana said, 'I am going to visit my friend, the Abbot of St Chariton's monastery.

دوست

Would you like to come with me?'

It didn't take her long to tighten her headscarf and put on her shoes. She knew of the monastery and of Maulana's friendship with the abbot but had never before accompanied him on his visits there.

The air was still cool when they left a few minutes later, Kimya carrying a jar of honey to take to the abbot. It was a good hour's walk to the monastery. They ambled through gardens and orchards where white and pink petals floated down like forgotten snowflakes, then followed a path that was soon shaded by rows of cypresses. When they arrived, the sun had reached the top of the trees and it was hot. An old monk in brown robes opened the wooden gate and led them through a dark corridor to an inner garden, itself surrounded by a cloister lined with finely carved colonnades. Behind the garden, but still in the precinct of the monastery, one could discern the dome of a small mosque, its minaret competing with the tapered shapes of two poplars growing next to it.

The abbot soon emerged from a room nearby. He, too, was clad in brown, with a wooden cross hanging on his chest. 'What a nice surprise,' he said, his eyes sparkling. 'And who is this young lady?' His face reminded Kimya of Father Chrisostom.

'This is Kimya,' Maulana said. 'Kimya has been living with us for some time now.'

She handed the abbot the jar of honey and he smiled a warm, happy smile.

'Would you like to stay in the garden while we talk?' the abbot suggested. 'Young girls are less prone to hurting themselves than boys,' he added, his smile widening, and Maulana laughed at the

دوست

memory of what had happened a few years earlier, when Ala ud din had fallen into a ravine nearby and been rescued, badly bruised, by the monks.

'St Chariton protected my son then,' he said. 'I'm sure he would protect Kimya too, but you're right, young girls take better care of themselves than young boys, and,' he added, laughing, 'one mosque in your monastery is enough.'

The abbot, too, started to laugh. The small mosque had been erected in thanksgiving to St Chariton for saving Ala ud din's life, a decision that had provoked angry comments among both Christians and Muslims. In their shared dislike for religious intolerance, Maulana and the abbot had ignored the comments and enjoyed their complicity.

The two men soon disappeared, leaving Kimya to herself. She sat down on a bench under the shade of a small willow. Peace suffused the garden, its silence broken from time to time only by the cooing of doves or a sudden flapping of wings. She let herself drift in the quiet of the moment, and closed her eyes. *Doost*. The word rose in her, as soft as the cooing of the birds.

'Would you like some water?'

Startled, she opened her eyes. A young monk was facing her, carrying a tray with a goblet of water. She thanked him and took the goblet. The water was cool and refreshing. She had not realised she was so thirsty. The young monk waited until she had finished but then, instead of leaving, he stared at her awkwardly.

'Are you Maulana's daughter?' he asked, blushing.

Maulana's daughter! She had never thought about her relationship with Maulana. She reflected for a moment. Maulana was

دوست

more than a father. He was something like Ahmed, her friend the hermit; he was also like Father Chrisostom. 'Maulana is not only a father,' she began, 'he is —' She was interrupted by the sound of foot-steps coming from the cloister. Turning her head, she saw the abbot and Maulana walking towards them. When she turned back again, the young monk, his question still hovering in the air, had vanished.

As they walked back to Konya she and Maulana remained silent, both lost in their thoughts. It was curious. She felt she had grown up in a way she couldn't quite understand.

Summer came once again, its scorching sun drawing everyone indoors or into the shade in search of coolness. In the squares, under the plane trees, old men dozed, from time to time brushing away a fly drunk from the heat. In the evening life returned, more vibrant for having been forced into retreat during the day. Cushions and kilims were brought on to the terraces, glasses of tea and dishes of sweetmeats appeared, and under the vault of a sky studded with stars, animated conversations took place, sometimes until dawn.

On Maulana's roof, like everywhere else, guests and visitors joined the family and talks and discussions went on until the children fell asleep and one by one the visitors disappeared.

One night, when Sultan Walad and Ala ud din had retired and the last guests had gone long ago, Maulana and Kerra, with Kimya fast asleep on her lap, were alone, the only two people, it seemed, still awake in the whole city now suspended in that stillness of the night when, according to Maulana, 'God is nearer and prayer reaches Him more easily.'

In the silence Maulana's voice rose, addressing some invisible presence. 'When the heart is sincere,' he was saying, 'help is at hand, wherever you are.' And to Kerra's dismay, her husband walked off the roof into the cool night air and vanished.

The muezzin was just starting the call to prayer when, hours later, Maulana walked back on to the terrace. Without a word he stood facing east, then prostrated himself.

'God is great,' he whispered. Kimya had woken up and she and Kerra joined in the prayer.

They were going down the narrow staircase that led to the main courtyard when Kerra noticed some fine white sand slipping out of Maulana's shoes.

'This sand is from the Hedjaz,' Maulana said. 'A traveller there had lost his way. I had to guide him back.'

Kimya looked out of the window and saw a grey sky. This meant the night would come even sooner. The autumn seemed to last for ever. She sighed, reflecting that there was still another moon to pass before the days would start to get longer. But then God had planned things well. True, light was scarce in the winter months, but then snow came, which wrapped everything in white stillness. The thought revived her and she started to cut the dough in front of her into small squares, placing a piece of meat in each one and then carefully folding them into triangles. She liked this kind of work that required attention and precision. She was so concentrated on her task that she didn't hear Kerra coming in.

'I wonder why Maulana hasn't come back from the college.' There was a slight worry in Kerra's voice. 'He should be back by now.' She sat down, adding as an afterthought, 'His friend

دوست

Sariduddin is waiting for him in the study.'

At that instant, Sultan Walad entered the kitchen. He was still wearing his coat and was out of breath. 'I told Sariduddin not to wait any longer. I don't think Father will come for a while.'

Kerra looked at him, alarmed. 'What makes you say that?'

Sultan Walad dropped his coat without answering then sat down beside Kerra, and Kimya started to prepare some tea.

'Early this morning,' Sultan Walad began, 'while Father was on his way to the public bath, something very strange happened. Father was surrounded as usual by a small crowd of students and followers and as they were passing near the sugar caravanserai, a man wrapped in a black cloak jumped out in front of him and took hold of his bridle.' Sultan Walad had stopped, clearly shaken at the memory. Kerra waited until he started again. 'The man and Maulana exchanged a few words, at which Maulana fainted and fell off his mule.'

Kerra put her hand to her mouth. 'Is he hurt? Is that why he hasn't come back?'

Sultan Walad shook his head. 'No, it's not that. Father is well. He recovered almost instantly. It's what followed that worries me.'

Kerra waited for him to explain.

'Well, I don't understand. Once Father had recovered, he took the man by the hand and together they went to Salah ud din Zarkob's house.' Sultan Walad frowned. 'And they are still there. It's very strange, as Father was supposed to talk at the college. I went there before coming here. There was already a large crowd. The people knew of the encounter and everybody was discussing it; they still thought Maulana would turn up, though. But he didn't!' Sultan Walad had said that with incredulity. 'The people began to

دوست

complain and, in the end, they left. Father's students are at a loss.'
He wiped his forehead with his hand. 'I don't know what to think
either.'

Kerra remained silent for a while. 'He will come back tonight,'
she said finally. 'Perhaps this man was bringing some important
news.'

Sultan Walad shook his head again. He was unconvinced.
'Delivering news doesn't take a whole day. It's something else, I
know. Something ...'

He didn't finish his sentence. He was still searching for words
when Ala ud din burst in. 'The man's name is Shams,' he cried
almost triumphantly, 'and he comes from Tabriz.' He was standing
with legs apart, a lock of hair falling over his brow.

'And how do you know all this?' Kerra asked, irritated at the way
the boy was boasting. Konya was fond of gossip, they all knew
that; but Kerra knew, too, that gossip not only distorts the truth, it
also soils those who spread it. She didn't let him answer her question.
'Enough! Your father knows what he is doing.' She got up and went
to the hearth where she started to rekindle the fire angrily while
Sultan Walad pushed Ala ud din towards the door.

Back at her task of folding the dough, Kimya repeated the name
she had just heard: 'Shams.' In Arabic it meant sun. So why this fear
at hearing the word? Outside a sudden gust of wind seemed to
answer her. She shuddered. 'Winter will soon be here,' she said.

Bent down over the fire, Kerra didn't reply.

The day dragged on until night fell. Still Maulana didn't return.
A narrow sliver of a moon had risen over the house and outside the
noise of the city had died down. They were all sitting in the kitchen

دوست

when Kerra suggested that Kimya and Sultan Walad went to Salah
ud din Zarkob's house and take some food with them.

Salah ud din was a goldsmith and a friend of Maulana. He lived
alone in a house only a few minutes away from Maulana's which,
since the death of his wife, had become too big for him. During the
day he worked in the bazaar where he had a tiny workshop.

Sultan Walad was walking ahead, holding an oil lamp. Except for
a cat, which ran away at their approach, the streets were empty.
They soon knocked at the door and Salah ud din opened it immediately. 'Ah, it's you,' he said. He didn't seem surprised to see them.
He was a small man with a square, sturdy body. Kimya had seen him
a few times among Maulana's visitors. Salah ud din was always
quiet, remaining mostly silent during the erudite discussions that
sometimes took place around Maulana. Nobody knew much about
him, except that he was a good man who could be trusted.

'They are in that far room,' he said, nodding in the direction of
a corridor leading to three doors, all closed. He hesitated. 'I don't
think we should disturb them.'

'We were wondering whether they needed some food,' Sultan
Walad said. 'It has been a long time since this morning.'

Salah ud din acquiesced silently, still unconvinced.

Kimya and Sultan Walad walked towards the furthest door. A
ray of light was flickering from under it. Sultan Walad set down the
lamp behind them, which now threw their two shadows towards the
door as if they were trying to get through it. There was not a sound
to be heard. They stood there for a few minutes, and then Sultan
Walad knocked hesitantly on the door. The idea of bringing food

here now seemed incongruous. The silence had deepened. Kimya looked at Sultan Walad. His face was very still. He brought his hand to his heart, then all at once bowed deeply towards the door. Curiously overtaken by a powerful wind that was blowing through her, Kimya closed her eyes. Then it all stopped and as she opened her eyes again, she saw Sultan Walad, pale and drained, holding the oil lamp and ready to go. Under the door, the light was still flickering. Without a word they pulled themselves away and as they left the house Kimya remembered Maulana showing her a magnet with several pieces of metal clinging to it. Tonight the magnet is behind that door, she thought, and I am one of the pieces of metal.

It was now over a week since the stranger had appeared. Maulana's house and Salah ud din's remained suspended in silence, life almost at a stop except for the evenings when Kimya walked to the door with the tray of food Kerra and she had prepared. It had almost become a ritual. She placed the tray near the door where the light kept its vigil and then sat down, breathing in the silence. Sometimes Sultan Walad joined her, sometimes Kerra. The food remained untouched. It had been tacitly agreed not to speak about Maulana and 'his new friend'.

'What is there to say?' Kerra had remarked. 'It's not for us to talk about it.' The stern determination in her voice commanded respect.

But Ala ud din could not restrain himself. 'Father's students are angry,' he said one day, returning from riding with his friends, full of the talk of the city.

Sultan Walad looked sad, but made no comment.

'They say,' Ala ud din went on, 'that this man, Shams, is just

108

دوست

another of those charlatans coming from the East to stir up trouble. They say that Father has abandoned them.' He paused and added with a trembling voice, 'I think he has abandoned us, too.'

'Ala ud din, hold your tongue.' Kerra's voice was sharp. 'That's not the way to talk about your father.'

The youth bent his head, and then walked out, leaving behind a trail of anger.

The days passed, interminable. The waiting became as tense as the string of a bow stretched to its utmost. One morning, Kimya dropped the pot she was carrying. It fell to the floor and burst into pieces.

'Couldn't you be more careful?' Kerra's voice was angry. Never before had Kimya seen her lose her temper. 'It doesn't matter, Kimya,' Kerra said almost immediately with a sad smile. 'It's not the pot I'm worried about.'

Together they gathered the broken pieces scattered over the floor. Those pieces are like the pieces of our hearts, Kimya thought. We can collect them and try to put them back together, yet the pot will never be the same.

The new moon rose, waxed and waned. The cold started to bite and the first snow shrouded the city, muffling its bustle to a whisper. Still Maulana and his friend remained secluded.

At first Maulana's absence had been felt as if he had gone on a journey. His laughter, his telling stories, the coming and going of his friends and students – all that was gone. It was almost unbearable; but one day, soon, he might be back. Yet as the days and weeks passed with Maulana still away from them, his presence felt closer. It seemed at times that he was behind the door, ready to burst in, just as in the autumn the horse chestnuts crack open, or in the spring the roses unfurl from their buds. Kerra was paler, but in her eyes was a restrained happiness. Looking at her, one thought of those pregnant women who, unhurried, let the world rush by, too busy with their own precious inner task to be ruffled by anything outside themselves. She calmly prepared the food she knew the two men locked in their room a few houses away wouldn't touch, and made sure there were always two sets of fresh clothes placed at their door. And she waited.

For Kimya, too, the shock and the sadness of the first days had been replaced by peace, a peace that every evening deepened in the silent wonder of her vigil at that door in Salah ud din's house. Those evenings had become her nourishment. They reverberated throughout the length of her days, giving her a sense of purpose. What that purpose was, though, she didn't know. Then one evening as she sat in her customary place a man – no doubt it was Shams – suddenly emerged from the room. Almost against her will, she looked up at him. His dark, burning eyes pierced through her fiercely, leaving nothing untouched, and she let out a cry. For a second the storm raged, followed by a stillness she had never felt before. When she opened her eyes, it was as if nothing had happened. In front of her, as usual, the door was closed with the same ray of light flickering under it. Entrenched in silence, the house was breathing quietly.

That night an angel of fire came to her in her dreams. 'Shams is here for you too,' the angel said. 'Today he has lifted a veil. The journey back has begun.'

She woke up, startled. What did it mean? she wondered. But she kept the dream to herself.

'Kimya, you mustn't be sad,' her friend Hatije said to her as they were walking through Qamar al din Garden, now shrouded in snow. Hatije was twelve years old, just like Kimya. She was the first close friend Kimya had ever had; even Nuran, the other girl with whom they played at times, didn't feel as close. Hatije had a round face and dark eyes, and was a little plump – 'from liking sweets too much,' Kimya teased her. Her father, a butcher, was among the most ardent of Maulana's followers.

'I'm not sad,' Kimya said. 'It's not that.'

'Then why do you not talk any more; why do you stay so much by yourself?'

'I'm trying to catch something,' Kimya said. An image came to her mind. 'It's like trying to pull a thread through the eye of a needle. You have to pay attention, you have to be very still, you have to concentrate.' She was getting excited. 'Yes,' she said, 'it's like when you try to get the thread through; you can't be distracted, you don't want to be distracted.'

Hatije was listening intently. 'Perhaps I understand,' she said, and she laughed, her wide, happy laugh. 'But I like to be distracted.'

Kimya couldn't help laughing too. Hatije was so honest, always herself, never pretending! She put her arm around her friend's shoulders. 'I love you, Hatije.' They went on walking slowly, silent for a while. 'But you see,' Kimya began again, 'I can't bear to be distracted, it's …' She paused. 'It's too powerful, it's so much what I long for.'

'But what is it that's so powerful, that you so much long for?'

دوست

'It's inside me.' Kimya had stopped walking. 'I don't know how
to explain. It's as if something is calling me and answering me at the
same time.' She shook her head. 'I don't understand it.' She pushed
the thoughts away as one would an importunate fly. 'It's getting cold;
let's go home,' she said.

The two girls retraced their steps, playing at putting their feet
back into their own footprints in the snow. They were progressing
slowly, then Hatije slipped. Kimya grasped her coat and they both
fell in the snow, where they lay laughing, unable to get back on their
feet.

'You see what I mean?' Kimya managed to stammer. 'One needs
to pay attention, and if one of us slips, then the other one slips too.'

They staggered to their feet and brushed off the white coldness
clinging to their kaftans. They looked at each other and burst into
another wave of laughter. All of a sudden there was a ringing in
Kimya's ears and everything around her became sharp, precise,
crystalline. She remained still, her laughter suspended. It was so
extraordinarily clear: this moment was as rich, as perfect as the
moments she spent in Salah ud din's house every evening. Life was
a whole, everything was connected, millions of snowflakes made only
one vast glorious mantle. Overwhelmed, she let herself drop full
length into the scattered snow. Hatije had stopped laughing too.
Concerned, she crouched down next to her friend and stared at her.
On an impulse, Kimya planted a kiss on her cheek. There was
nothing to worry about. They looked at each other and started to
giggle again.

'You look a nice mess, the two of you, and, I must say, a rather happy mess!' Kerra exclaimed when the two girls entered the kitchen, still laughing. 'I haven't seen such red cheeks for a long time. What about some hot milk?'

The following day Maulana and his friend came out of their retreat.

# – XIV –

IT WAS EARLY MORNING. THE SKY WAS JUST TURNING INTO that cold white grey that precedes the return of the light. Alone in the kitchen, Kerra was rekindling the fire when she heard the sound of footsteps behind her. She looked over her shoulder and there was her husband standing in the doorway. He was pale and so thin that he seemed to be floating in his robe but in his eyes the fierceness and, yes, the joy quietly shining were unmistakable. For a second Jalal, her husband, the man everyone called Maulana, lowered his gaze as if shy to let her see too much, yet unable to hold back a fleeting smile: like a spring breeze caressing his lips, she thought. She couldn't help noticing the dark marks under his eyes. Unwittingly she mirrored him and lowered her gaze. 'So you're happy,' her smile was saying, 'and my heart swells with the joy of your joy.' Then she became aware of the large, tall shape over-shadowing her husband.

Jalal turned round. 'This is Shams ud din, the confidant of my soul,' he said softly.

She remained silent. Never had she seen her husband look so vulnerable. He was like a small child, abandoned, full of wonder. He paused for a moment and added, 'You must treat him as the most precious part of my being.'

He had almost whispered the last words as if they could not

دوست

really convey the magnitude of his feelings. The man had stepped forward as Jalal was talking. She thought of a great tree, powerful, majestic, protective. He had dark, unsmiling eyes, full of a fire so intense that she gasped and her heart jumped in her chest as if trying to escape. The man let go of her eyes and bowed deeply to her. So this was Shams. Who was he? The question rose burning in her mind, and remained unanswered. She was still staring at the two men in front of her, trying to think of something to say, when Shams turned round and walked away, Jalal on his heels. The whole scene had lasted hardly a few minutes and, alone again, she was wondering if she had not dreamed it when Kimya came in, breathless.

'Maulana and his friend have come out of their retreat. They are here; I saw them entering Maulana's study.'

So it was not a dream after all. She nodded. 'I know. At last they have come out, and I'm glad, but Kimya ...' She hesitated. 'I'm also frightened.' She was shivering.

Alarmed, Kimya took off her shawl and folded it around Kerra's shoulders. 'Is it this man, Shams?'

But Kerra had already composed herself. She shook her head. 'I don't know what came over me; don't listen to me, Kimya. I am only worried that these two are not paying the least attention to their well-being.' She sighed. 'Men go too far, they lose track of this world, then it all falls to us women.' She could feel her irritation mounting, replacing the awesome fear she had just experienced, and that was somehow a relief. But she knew she was letting herself fall into easy clichés, away from her own truth.

Silently they busied themselves with the various tasks of the morning, getting some more wood for the fire, putting water to boil, peeling vegetables …

'Perhaps now they will start to eat again,' Kerra said, her voice ringing with resentment at the thought of all the food she'd had to give away for the last – she counted to herself – yes, for the last six weeks. Then she laughed. Why be angry? The food had not been wasted; quite a few beggars had been fed and, though he might be thin, her husband was happy.

'Kimya, you mustn't listen to me,' she said again. 'God's gifts are often difficult to appreciate; nevertheless they are gifts.'

At that moment the sun flooded the room as though acknowledging that fear or anger were merely clouds hiding the glory of the sun. Their eyes met in silent complicity. Something new, something still unknown but powerful, had entered the house. Out of Kimya's lips a song sprang, the same song Farokh had sung that evening by the fire when Father Chrisostom had visited the village for the last time: wild, glorious, a hymn to the gift of life, a song that, unknown to her till this moment, had remained with her, its origin lost somewhere in the steppes of Central Asia. Startled, Kerra dropped the squash she was cleaning. Somehow the song was bringing back the dark, unsmiling eyes of Shams. And again she shivered.

Winter softened its grip, once again the almond trees started to burst into clouds of pink, and out of the silence of the previous weeks emerged the whisper of a new life. Maulana and Shams, their seclusion and their fast now over, were inseparable – either sitting for hours in Maulana's study or going out on various errands. At times Sultan Walad or a few of Maulana's friends joined the two men, and

دوست

to Kerra's relief the trays of food prepared for them no longer returned untouched. Only Ala ud din kept his distance. He was angry with his father for 'abandoning them' as he put it, and made sure that everybody knew it. When at home he slammed the doors, frowned and refused to answer questions, using the smallest pretext to burst into a blind rage, and the rest of the time he rode furiously on the *maidan* with his friends.

In Konya curiosity had not abated. People observed Maulana and Shams going to the mosque, the bazaar or the public baths, sometimes talking animatedly, sometimes sunk into silence, and they wondered: What was this invisible barrier that made those two men unapproachable? A barrier that was fiercely guarded by Shams's glare – while Maulana, his attention fixed on Shams, seemed unaware of the world around him. The people looked at the great teacher everyone had once revered and could not believe their eyes. Thin, childlike, he was a mere shadow of himself.

Maulana's students, for their part, became bitter. They had expected their Master to start his lectures again at the college, but they now realised he had no intention of doing so. Maulana was not the religious teacher they had known. Lost was his composure, lost was his look of dignified austerity. They saw him at times laughing without restraint, at times crying, equally without restraint. Kimya heard the people whispering: 'Is Maulana going mad? What is this man, Shams, doing to him?' They once saw Maulana running home and another time, even worse, whirling on the corner of a street while two small children clapped their hands and Shams stood by, eyes closed, lost in some dream of his own. Later on, Kimya asked Maulana, 'Why were you turning? What does it do to you?'

117

'It takes the heart closer to God,' Maulana answered. 'It is a very ancient custom. It belongs to the science of man, the science that allows men to find their way back to God. It was perfected in Persia long before the Prophet.' His face had softened. 'Shams introduced me to it,' he said.

'Can I turn, too?' she asked.

'Not yet, Kimya, not yet.' He was shaking his head and his eyes were full of tenderness. 'Turning can harm those who are not ready for it.'

She must have looked puzzled.

'It's quite simple,' he said. 'This turning touches the heart; it brings up powerful emotions, often confused with high spiritual states; then the temptation to turn becomes great. That, however, will only hamper the spiritual development of those who indulge in it for their own emotional satisfaction. This is why it has been kept secret for so long.' He paused and seemed to fall into his own thoughts. 'Before turning, the heart has to be stripped of all attachments,' he said after a while, then in a whisper he added, 'Not everyone is willing to be burned to that extent.'

Afterwards she wondered. What did he mean? What she felt for Maulana, for Kerra, was that attachment? Wasn't that love?

As time went on, some of Maulana's students approached Sultan Walad. 'Tell your father that without the light of his teaching, life is unendurable for us. Tell him that without the balm of his wisdom, we are like blind men stumbling in the dark.'

Sultan Walad listened to their complaints. But what could he do? 'I hardly see my father these days,' he told them, 'and when I see him, it's only to watch over him and Shams.' How could he explain

دوست

the intensity of the silence he sometimes shared with Shams and his father? How could he tell them that, within the walls of the small study where the two men spent so much of their time, there was more life than in the whole city of Konya and beyond? They looked at him with suspicion. Was Sultan Walad betraying them like his father? And all this because this dervish, this Qalandar, like so many of those wandering heretics who brought only disorder and blasphemy wherever they went, had taken hold of Maulana's mind!

The abomination caused by Shams became even more clearly evident when one day it was reported that Maulana had visited the Jewish quarter and there had bought a whole gourd of wine.

'Surely this is only malevolent gossip,' one of the students exclaimed. 'It can't be true!'

But after investigation it appeared that earlier in the day Maulana had gone to his old Jewish friend, Joshua, the wine merchant, and asked if he could buy a gourd of wine from him. At first Joshua had thought it was a joke. How could a Muslim, and a religious teacher at that, ask for wine? But Maulana was serious.

'This is the request of my beloved Shams; I do not question his requests,' he had said, and Joshua had given him a gourd of his best wine while refusing to be paid.

'May the Lord of the Universe protect you,' Joshua had told him and Maulana had smiled back at him. 'Such a smile!' Joshua said. 'A smile that brought the entire sun into my poor, miserable shop.'

'What did I tell you?' one of the students exclaimed. Hassan was a young lad of about sixteen, a friend of Ala ud din with whom he often rode on the *maidan*. 'Our Master is possessed,' he said. 'This Shams is doing Shaitan's work.'

دوست

Somehow Hassan's words expressed what all the students suspected: Shams was evil; not only was he depriving them of the presence and teaching of their Master but, much worse, he had ensnared Maulana and was taking him away from God. They were indignant.

Kimya was sweeping the courtyard when Maulana came home carrying the gourd. It was a sunny day, still cool but full of the promises of spring. He stroked her head as he walked by, then went rapidly to his study. As he opened the door she heard Shams's voice: 'Good, my friend. This wine is, in more than one way, for the glory of God.'

A few moments later, the two men came out and sat in the sun on the old stone bench attached to the western wall, a few steps away from where Kimya was still sweeping. She noticed the gourd resting on Shams's lap and was going to leave when he stopped her. 'You don't need to go,' he said. She hesitated. Was he asking her to stay? Uncertain, she sat down in the doorway and looked at the two men. Without paying attention to her any more, Shams took the gourd and pulled out the cork and then, slowly, deliberately, he poured the wine into the narrow gutter that ran around the courtyard. He poured until the gourd was almost empty and then, taking a tin cup out of his robe, filled it half full of wine.

'Idols must be broken,' he said, bringing the cup to his lips and, having taken a sip, he offered the cup to Maulana who, in his turn, brought it to his lips.

'Idols are the crutches men take for real and then lean on,' Shams went on. His voice, low and deep, seemed to emerge from his belly rather than from his throat. 'Reputation is one of these idols, and so are rules and habits.' He sounded angry but then, to Kimya's surprise, he laughed and exclaimed, 'Today, my friend, you've broken a few idols.'

Maulana was smiling. 'Drinking from the cup that has touched the lips of the Friend is sweeter than all the wine in the world,' he said.

A bird suddenly flew over and sat in the chestnut tree near the southern wall. It was a soft blue-grey with white marks on its wings. Stretching its throat, it started to send forth trills with all its strength. Kimya felt curiously moved. Such intensity in such a small creature!

Shams turned towards her. 'You see, knowingly or unknowingly all beings have within themselves the desire to praise.' Still talking, he stood up and, eyes closed, started to whirl slowly, his arms folded over his chest.

In the market the next day Kimya heard that Shams was the devil and 'How terrible it must be to live with him in the same house!' She walked away, ignoring the remarks, but her heart felt heavy. She wanted to cry out, 'It's not like that at all. Shams is no devil, he is a great wind, igniting everything he touches; he is the carrier of unspoken news, he ...' She felt a tearing inside and stopped in her stride, gasping for air. The stalls around her seemed to sway and her heart was beating too fast.

Then she felt someone taking her hand and heard Kerra's voice, so soft, so calm. 'Let's go home, it's getting late.'

'What happened?' Kimya asked later as she was sitting in the kitchen with Kerra, a glass of tea in her hand.

'Your body is growing, and so is your soul,' Kerra said. 'It can be overwhelming at times. But that is a great gift, even though it is sometimes difficult to bear.' She paused, and then added as though talking to herself, 'Things are changing very fast at the moment.'

A few days later, while sitting in the courtyard preparing vegetables for the evening meal, Kimya reflected that this was true: things were changing. Things had already changed. Some invisible power, some secret fragrance had taken hold of Maulana's house, altering the very fibres of everyday life. She was picking out a leek from the basket at her feet when she heard footsteps. Looking up, she was surprised to see Shams entering the courtyard.

He walked towards her and then asked, 'May I sit with you?' His voice was soft, without any trace of the imperiousness she was accustomed to – though his eyes, as piercing as ever, aroused the usual flow of conflicting emotions in her.

She nodded her assent, surprised that he had asked. He sat down at a distance and remained silent, his head bent over his lap. She became aware of the sounds of the city, muffled by the walls around them. The quietness of the courtyard was now suffused with power. Unable to continue with her task, she asked, 'Is Tabriz like Konya?'

He raised his head. 'Tabriz is a city of blue mosques and bright skies,' he said pensively, as if talking to himself. 'Konya is a city of light.'

She waited for him to explain, but instead he continued, 'The roses of Tabriz are small and pale yellow, and their hearts are

دوست

bleeding. There are no roses like that yet in Konya. But one day there will be.'

She felt her heart leap in her chest and, shivering, she let the knife she was holding slip out of her hands. His words carried a message she could not yet decipher.

Ignoring her reaction, he went on, 'There are quarters in Tabriz from where the souls of saints rise at night. They gather in groups as red and green doves, then they fly to Mecca where they circle round the Kaaba.'

She stared at him. What an astonishing thing to say! She knew only of grey pearly doves and had never heard of green or red doves. A furtive smile, like a passing cloud, hovered over his lips. He seemed to be looking beyond her. She pondered: Was Shams a red or a green dove?

To her unspoken question, he replied, 'There are people in Tabriz in comparison to whom I am nothing.' Then he stood up. 'Remember the roses of Tabriz,' he said. 'They are close to God, for only a bleeding heart can find Him.' He seemed to reflect for a while and then continued, 'Men don't want to know this and they quickly forget it. And when their heart is called and when it bleeds, they complain instead of giving thanks.' His eyes sharpened and bored into hers. 'But you, Kimya, you won't forget.' And before she knew it, he had turned away and disappeared into the house, leaving her trembling and more confused than ever.

In the days and then the weeks that followed, she found that whatever menial task she was involved with, Shams's eyes never ceased to follow her, and also that she was enfolded at all times in

دوست

a strange stillness. Her tasks acquired a different quality, becoming acts of praise and devotion. She discovered, too, that time couldn't be relied upon any more. Sometimes the simplest action seemed to last for ever, though when she looked at the shadows on the walls she could see that only a few minutes had passed. At other times it seemed as though a minute or so had elapsed when in fact hours had gone by. Life was not a succession of unrelated moments any more. It was more like a melody confidently unfolding, each note attached to the next in subtle harmony. The melody, in its beauty and simplicity, could never be foreseen, yet each note came never a second too early, never a second too late and, perhaps more surprisingly, it was always the right note. Yet each one had to be caught as one catches a bird in full flight. It left her exhilarated and breathless, never sure of what was to come.

Thus life became music and then, of course, the musicians made their entrance. One evening a man was invited to come to Maulana's house with his *ney*. That night out of Maulana's house a sound arose which was as fine and subtle as the breath, calling, begging, at turns plaintive, at turns joyful. In the street outside, people stopped as they passed.

'Where is this music coming from?' they asked. Then they whispered to each other that, yes, it was coming from Maulana's house.

'Music! In Maulana's house!' they murmured. 'He who used to say that music was a distraction from God!' And once again, the citizens of Konya shook their heads in dismay.

In Maulana's study, Kimya was slipping into some unknown yet familiar world. On her cheek the cushion on which she was resting

124

her head was rough and smelled of smoke. Somewhere in the distance Maulana's voice was growing faint. She could hear the sound of glasses ringing against the copper tray, Shams's heavy coughing at times and, behind it all, the sound of the *ney* now ascending, now expanding, then for a second remaining suspended until it turned on itself and became one long, penetrating note. From time to time she opened her eyes, catching sight of the flames leaping and dropping in the hearth as if following the music. The night stretched and the moon journeyed through the sky, while the boundaries between sleep and wakefulness, between herself and the loss of herself, became thinner than a veil.

Just before the call to prayer, the music stopped. A few muffled sounds told her the musicians and the guests were leaving. The last sound she heard was the birds chattering with the first intimation of dawn.

A few days later, as she was on her way out, she overheard Shams talking to Sultan Walad. The two men were coming out of Maulana's study and didn't notice her.

'I don't care about people talking and complaining. That's not the point,' Shams said. His voice was forceful, but not angry. 'I don't care that they dislike me, you know that. But if my presence causes discord in this city, then I will have to go.'

She stopped, alarmed. Shams going away! It was true that his presence was causing hostility and anger, but to the point of making him leave! Yet Shams never talked for the sake of talking. What he said, he meant. She walked away, feeling suddenly sad, her heart heavy. I do not want him to go, she thought, surprised at herself.

# – XV –

AKBAR HAD JUST TURNED SEVENTEEN AND HE WAS CONFUSED. He was a tall young man with dark eyes, dark hair and an air of confidence that made his friends believe he knew more than he really did. For years, as a child, he had heard of the great teacher, Jalal ud din, who gave talks in the madrassa about God and how to reach Him. He had seen him sometimes going through the streets of Konya with his students and had been among the children who followed him, hoping that one day he too would be among his students. And now he was. For the last two years he had attended Maulana's lectures while starting to study law; that is, examining the ways of men, their dilemmas and their conflicts through the words of God and through the interpretations of wise and holy men. Akbar's world was an orderly one where life was clear and simple. One acknowledged that there was one God only and that Mohammed was his prophet, one prayed five times a day, one gave alms, one fasted on the holy month of Ramadan, and, God willing, one would one day go on pilgrimage to Mecca.

But now where did he stand? The clear boundaries that had defined his life were becoming increasingly blurred. Maulana, the respected religious teacher who had been his role model, couldn't be relied on any more – or so it seemed. Akbar's fellow students accused Maulana of having forgotten his duties and, worse, of

126

دوست

flouting religion. Akbar now spent his nights crying and torturing his mind in vain, trying to make sense of what made no sense. He felt abandoned, lost, betrayed. To whom could he turn? Sharing his feelings with his friends didn't help. Like him, they were confused, angry and worried. Some of them had asked the imam for advice, only to be told to forget about Maulana and to turn to God. But somehow, that didn't bring them relief. It was as if God Himself had abandoned them – a frightening thought, close to blasphemy, which made Akbar fall into an even darker despair.

One morning, after another sleepless night, he thought of someone who could possibly help: Sadruddin Qonavi. The man was highly respected, his reputation beyond reproach. Several years ago, he had met the Great Sheikh, Ibn el Arabi, and later had married his daughter. It was also known that, after a rather stormy encounter with Maulana, the two men had come to realise that they shared a common understanding of God and His creation, and they had become close friends.

Sadruddin lived on the outskirts of Konya. His house, small and whitewashed, was hidden among orchards, and it took Akbar some time to find it. Sadruddin himself opened the door. He seemed surprised to see Akbar.

'What can I do for you, my son?'

Sadruddin looked older than Akbar had expected. His back was bent and his face, partly hidden by a neatly cut beard, was deeply lined.

'Come in, come in,' Sadruddin invited.

Akbar entered, not quite sure why he was here any more. The house smelled of candle and oil. Sadruddin ushered him into a small room furnished with only a few cushions and two worn-out carpets.

دوست

'Do sit down,' Sadruddin said, waiting for his guest to say something. Sadruddin himself sat down, closed his eyes, and for a minute Akbar wondered if the man had not fallen asleep.

'I came to ask you for advice,' Akbar finally said.

Sadruddin opened his eyes and gave Akbar a deep look, but still he said nothing.

'I, I don't know what to do,' Akbar stammered. Thoughts were swirling in his head, his heart was pounding. 'It's Maulana,' he managed to utter, and then stopped, unable to continue.

'Ah . . .' Sadruddin's voice trailed off, and he sighed.

The silence had taken on a different quality. It was as though the room were pulsing.

Sadruddin leaned back against the wall and pulled his jacket closer around his chest. 'The world is not black and white, my son,' he said. 'Have you not yet discovered that it's made of many hues of grey, and' – he laughed and his face brightened – 'of many other colours?'

Akbar frowned. What did he mean? What kind of enigma was Sadruddin offering him?

'You think in terms of good and bad, of right and wrong, of reward and punishment,' Sadruddin went on, 'but this is the world of childhood!' His face was animated and he looked curiously younger. 'Little boys play hide and seek,' he continued. 'They ride wooden horses and use wooden swords. Is this what you are still at?' The tone of his voice was stern, yet full of humour.

Akbar felt the blood rising to his cheeks.

Sadruddin pretended not to notice. 'There comes a time when, faced with the unacceptable, the heart must accept it.' He paused for

دوست

a moment and added, as an afterthought, 'This is the test, for the food of the heart is not made of either/or. It embraces all. Do you understand?'

Akbar felt ill at ease. He had come for advice and what he was given was incomprehensible to him. He remained silent.

'The heart wants to embrace all,' Sadruddin repeated, his hands holding an invisible sphere. 'It cannot do with only one side of the cake.' Sadruddin laughed again, a young laugh. 'It wants it all, the good and the bad, the joy and the pain, and it knows nothing of reward and punishment. Can you conceive of such a thing?'

Akbar was at a loss, his world turned upside down.

Sadruddin took pity on him. 'Don't try to understand.' His eyes had softened. 'Understanding will come later. You came for advice and here is my advice: Stand back and accept.' Sadruddin's voice had taken on a strange fierceness. 'Accept that you don't understand anything of what is going on around you.' He was hammering the words with his hands. 'Accept that you have no way of even imagining what is happening. And accept your pain, too.' Again he paused. 'And thank God for it.' He remained silent for a while, letting Akbar digest what he had just said.

'Do you know that learning takes many shapes, even the shape of non-learning?' Sadruddin asked casually.

Akbar stared at his host, frightened. Each question Sadruddin was putting to him tore at the root of everything he knew, everything he believed in.

'Our Master has entered the world of no dimension,' Sadruddin went on, 'and, God willing, those who love him will enter it in their turn.' Sadruddin put his hand on Akbar's arm. 'Unknown to you,

دوست

my son, a treasure is on its way and, God willing, one day it will reach your shore. But remember, pain must be woven together with the threads of love and patience. Don't ever let pain poison you. A beautiful carpet is not woven in one day. You're just at the beginning.'

Akbar was shaken. The sparks in Sadruddin's eyes were rekindling the fire Maulana had once lit. He suddenly felt like crying. 'My heart is thirsty,' he said, abandoning all pretence.

Sadruddin nodded. 'Have you ever considered that this very thirst is the gift that is taking you to God?'

Akbar closed his eyes. The words, unexpected and shocking though they were, felt like a balm to his heart.

'Quenching your thirst is God's work, not Maulana's, or mine for that matter. And that work,' he added, 'will take what it takes; that is, everything.'

A knock at the door interrupted Sadruddin.

He put his hand on Akbar's shoulder. 'Keep your love for Maulana untainted and you will see in time that all is well. And remember, patience.' He had pronounced the last word slowly as men do when teaching a child a new word. He laughed again, and stood up. 'This is a word, I know, that is not entrancing to the young.' The meeting was over. Followed by Akbar, he went to the door.

A girl was standing on the doorstep, with something in her hands wrapped in a blue cloth.

'Ah, it's you, Kimya,' Sadruddin exclaimed.

'Here are some *tarhanas* for you to enjoy,' Kimya said, offering him the small bundle of bulgur cakes.

Sadruddin turned towards Akbar. 'Have you met Kimya?' he enquired.

130

Akbar hesitated. He had often seen Kimya around, but never talked to her. Young men don't mix with girls. He shook his head, indicating that he had not. But he knew that Kimya was Ala ud din's sister and that she was part of Maulana's household. He looked at her with a new curiosity. The light in her eyes reminded him of Maulana's eyes. They held the same light.

'How is Maulana?' Sadruddin asked.

Kimya's face lit up. 'Maulana is well,' she said and then, looking down at her feet, she added softly, 'He is happy.'

This time Akbar noticed her eyelashes, long and curved. How strange! The intensity of his exchange with Sadruddin seemed to have manifested itself in the shape of this young girl.

'I must go,' he said brusquely and, having bowed to Sadruddin, he walked away.

He was not sure whether he was fleeing or dancing. He had come in search of advice and certainty and instead the little he knew – or thought he knew – had been taken away from him. He was left empty-handed, and yet he felt curiously happy. Oh, he was still in the dark; more than ever, in fact, but at the end of the tunnel, far in the distance, there was the hint of a light. And that light was the same he had once experienced around Maulana, the same he had seen again this very day, in both Sadruddin's and Kimya's eyes.

As he approached the main square with its fountain and its plane trees in their newly born greenness, he saw a group of his friends sitting on the steps of the mosque. They were discussing something animatedly. On an impulse he turned away and entered the first narrow lane on his left. Sadruddin's words were still ringing in his ears: 'Don't ever let pain poison you.'

'I won't,' he whispered to himself. 'I won't.'

## XVI

MORE THAN A YEAR HAD ELAPSED. IT SEEMED A LONG TIME since Alim had been stumbling around, proud of showing off his new ability to walk. He now ran beside Kerra and Kimya wherever they went, and again spring was turning into summer. Soon the days of scorching heat would be back and with them the long evenings stretching into coolness. Already the gardens were exploding into patches of colour and once again in the late after-noons, like today, Kimya and Hatije met under the shade of the poplars of Qamar al din Garden. They were walking in silence along a path lined with roses and fragrant with their scent. It was that time before sunset and before prayer when the hustle and bustle of the day slowly comes to a rest as the light softens and the birds assemble for their evening concert.

Kimya stretched her arms, enjoying the moment. It had been a long, full day. There had been the usual tour of the market, then after feeding Alim and taking him to a neighbour, she and Kerra had gone to visit a bed-ridden woman on the other side of the city. Together they had cleaned the house, made some soup and sat beside the bed where the woman was lying. She was old. Her husband killed a long time ago in an accident, her children dead before their time, she had no one to take care of her except Kerra and some kind neighbours. And now she was ill, 'tired of living', she said. Her eyes anxiously searching Kerra's, she asked, 'Will I be reunited with my husband and my sons? Tell me, what does Maulana say?'

Kerra pressed the woman's hand. 'Of course you will be together again.' Maulana often asserted that love was the river of eternal life. 'Your love for your husband and your sons, and their love for you, are a river,' she said. 'That river is carrying all of you towards the same ocean.'

The woman had shut her eyes; two big tears were running down her cheeks. A great peace, like the wings of a large bird or the folds of Shams's cloak – why should that image cross Kimya's mind? – had spread over the room. The woman seemed asleep. Around them the stillness was tingling with invisible sparks. They let the silence expand until Kerra disengaged her hand, and quietly they left the house. They walked home silently, still filled with the peace of the room.

'That was beautiful,' Kimya said as they reached the house.

As she pushed open the door and stepped in, Kerra turned towards Kimya: 'Love takes you by surprise, doesn't it?'

Love! Was it love, that peace she had experienced at the woman's bedside? Kimya kept wondering while attending to her usual tasks of bringing in water, preparing dumplings for the evening meal and collecting the clothes that had dried in the sun during the afternoon. The sense of peace had been overwhelming; it had also made her feel refreshed and immensely grateful. It was somehow similar to what she had felt during those nights spent sitting at the door of the room where Maulana and Shams had retired. It was the same feeling that at times made her sing with joy and at others made her cry with a desperate yearning. Love! Was this what it was?

دوست

She was still thinking about it as Hatije and she followed the paths of Qamar al din Garden. They wandered through the alleys for a while and then sat on the edge of the small pool in the centre of the garden. Above them the leaves of a poplar shimmered in the breeze, while in the water, caught by the sun, the fish sent indecipherable messages in red and gold flashes. Kimya stretched, enjoying the moment, and let her hand brush the surface of the water.

Hatije looked at her friend with curiosity. 'Is it true that Maulana is planning a concert in Ana Khatun's garden?' she asked. 'My mother heard about it in the bazaar. But one hears so many things in the bazaar,' she added, half laughing.

'Oh, it's true.' Kimya raised her hand and let shiny drops of water rain back into the pool. 'Ana has heard about Maulana's new love of music, and she has offered her garden for a concert. And, you know, her friend, Taous, will play the harp and sing.'

'Taous!' Hatije exclaimed. 'But she used to be a prostitute!' Hatije was alarmed. 'I know that last year she threw herself at the feet of Maulana and people say she amended her ways, but still!'

Kimya shrugged. 'People say! People say! They also say that her singing makes them cry and keeps them awake at night. The truth is that Taous and Ana are holy women, and Maulana told us it will be a beautiful evening. Will you come?'

Hatije didn't answer. She had become suddenly serious: 'It's true that people talk,' she said. 'They are shocked at the way Maulana is behaving. They say Shams is taking him away from God.' She hesitated. 'And now a concert with women, and with Taous! What will they say this time?'

Kimya shut her eyes for a second. There it was again: the gossips,

دوست

the incomprehension, the hostility. She felt a burst of anger, then shrugged it away. 'Well, people will continue to complain and grumble, of course,' she said matter-of-factly. 'They have no love in their hearts; that's why they complain.'

'Is that what you think?' Hatije was curious. 'You live with Maulana, you're part of his family. Tell me, with Shams now living with you, how is it? It cannot be easy.'

Kimya looked at her friend, grateful to be asked. 'It is difficult,' she admitted. 'I miss Maulana. He used to be with us much more; he used to tell us stories, to make me read the Qoran; he corrected my Persian. Now we hardly see him; he spends most of his time with Shams. And then, as you know, outside there is the gossip, there are the complaints!' She sighed. 'People don't understand. How could they?' A bird flew over the pool, distracting them for a while.

'You know,' Kimya went on, 'Shams is not the monster people imagine. We were warm and comfortable with Maulana and it's true that now it's not so comfortable, but something new is at work, something …' She hesitated, then shut her eyes, trying to capture the essence of that something. 'Something is changing,' she said in the end. 'Shams is changing us. In what way, I don't know yet …'

She was still talking when a high-pitched sound pierced her ears. The strange thing was that it was coming from within, clearly intended for her only, and clearly a warning. 'Stop,' the sound intimated. 'These are things that words must not sully.'

They remained silent for a while. In the distance they could hear the voices of children at play and the rhythmic sound of a horse ambling along. A donkey started to bray. She looked at Hatije who

دوست

sat next to her, unaware of what had happened yet so full of goodwill, always so loyal. She pressed her hand and Hatije smiled her happy, trusting smile in return. The sun, now low behind the trees, was brushing the garden with gold. Kimya stood up. The sound in her ears had stopped as quickly as it had come. 'Will you come to the concert?' she asked again. 'Will your parents come?'

Hatije looked uncertain. 'I don't know. I'm not sure.'

They walked slowly out of the garden. The glow of the oil lamps in the shops gave the streets an air of festivity. Soon the call to prayer would resound over the city. As they passed a group of young men, one of them called out.

'Kimya, Hatije, wait for me, I'm coming with you.'

It was Ala ud din. The two girls stopped and waited for a while. Kimya noticed that Akbar, the young man she had met at Sadruddin's door, was among the youths. He looked ill at ease. As they were standing there, they heard one of them exclaim angrily: 'I tell you Shams must leave, or we will never have our teacher back.' It was Hassan, Ala ud din's closest friend. The two girls looked at each other. The words were like an echo of their conversation.

'Let's go,' Kimya said brusquely, and they started to walk away, soon caught up by Ala ud din.

'Why didn't you wait for me?' he asked.

'It's getting late,' Kimya said, 'and I don't like some of your friends.'

'You mean you don't like what they say. But they're right—'

She interrupted him. 'Ala ud din, I know what you think, I know what your friends think, and I don't want to hear it.' She was astonished at herself. She had never talked like that to Ala ud din.

دوست

He too was taken by surprise. He stood in the middle of the lane looking shocked. Kimya and Hatije were already several steps ahead.

'Who do you think you are?' he shouted. Disturbed in its sleep, a dog started to bark. 'Stupid girls!' he exclaimed, kicking a stone that went rolling down the lane.

Planning the concert in Ana's garden had not been easy. At first Sultan Walad had questioned the whole idea of the concert.

'Don't you know, Father, that it will feed the anger of your enemies?'

'Of course,' Maulana had answered. 'But anything would feed their anger. What they are after is their own sense of righteousness. As for music, I myself was deaf to it until my soul, awakened by the light of my beloved Shams, heard what it couldn't hear before. Perhaps such music will take the cotton out of their ears, at least for some of them.'

Then Taous had refused to sing and play the harp in public. 'My singing is for Him,' she had said, 'and for no one else.'

But Maulana had replied that the love of God was contagious and that, more than words, music and songs in praise of Him were sparks that could set hearts aflame, and Taous had relented, but on one condition: no one would set eyes on her while she sang. Maulana had agreed.

And so the obstacles had been removed, and tonight the concert was taking place.

The night was warm and fragrant with the scent of jasmine. In a sky

138

دوست

of dark silk, a waxing moon was keeping watch. A platform had been erected and on it a carpet spread for the musicians. All around cushions had been arranged for the audience to sit on while, disseminated through the garden, oil lamps caught here a face, here the shine of a kaftan, here the greenness of a bush.

Slowly a small crowd was assembling: friends of Maulana such as Sadruddin Qonavi, Namj al Razi, Salah ud din Zarkob, the goldsmith, and some younger men, friends of Sultan Walad and – Kimya felt grateful for this – a few of Maulana's students, those who wouldn't condemn him for not teaching them any more. Among them was Akbar who averted his eyes when he noticed that she was looking at him. It was curious, she thought, the place was buzzing, but not so much with the chatting of people – their voices were muffled as if they were afraid to speak too loudly – as with expectation. She could sense a tension in the air, a mixture of anticipation and apprehension. She caught sight of Hatije sitting in the front row with her mother. She too was quiet. So they had come after all! Kimya was glad. Not far from them Ana Khatun, the owner of the garden, with her eyes closed, had retreated to a world of her own. Close to her Kerra was waving, indicating that there was room beside her. Kimya made her way through the crowd and sat between Kerra and a small fountain that sent droplets of coolness on to her arm.

She had hardly sat down when Maulana entered the garden accompanied by Shams. The two men took their seats in front of the platform and the small assembly fell silent. Then there came the sound of footsteps and from behind the bushes the musicians appeared: a man with several *neys* of different sizes, another one with two *tanburs* and a third with a *rebab*, all of them wearing dark blue kaftans over black baggy trousers. They sat down on the platform and, taking no notice of the audience, started tuning their instruments.

But where was Taous? People began to whisper. Had she refused to come? Had the idea of a woman performing in front of a mixed assembly been finally rejected? The musicians began to play and slowly the shuffling and the whispers died away. Kimya noticed that Maulana had closed his eyes as the music now filled the night. She felt the garden expanding and soon time too lost its hold. She let herself sink into the music and was startled when it stopped and the whispering began again. She heard a woman asking, 'Is Taous not to appear at all?' The musicians had put their instruments aside and seemed to be taking a rest. People looked at Maulana; he was sitting motionless, eyes still closed. Next to him, Shams was rubbing his chin, apparently lost in his thoughts.

Then, coming as though from nowhere, notes like drops of water sprang up and cascaded into the night. The sound was coming from behind the musicians, fresh, crystalline, then out of the music a voice rose as pure as the water of the mountain streams. It was more than a voice: it was a beam of light piercing the night; it was a fragrance one could breathe. It flooded Kimya, making her body vibrate. Then it became a sharp blade and she gasped. She was the voice; she was each note rising in the night. She ascended then bent, begged, lamented, rose again, now filled with unbearable joy, now broken by unbearable pain. She was the current of pure water, she was the strings of the harp, she was torn apart and made whole, all at the same time. Then everything disappeared.

دوست

The cold on her forehead brought her back. Somewhere above her was Kerra's voice sounding worried. 'Kimya, are you all right?' She opened her eyes. The night had lost its shine and Kerra was pressing a wet cloth on her brow. Her eyes were saying, 'I know, I know. Sometimes it's too much to bear.'

Kimya remembered the day when she had cried in the hollow of a tree, unable to explain what it was she had experienced. This time, there was no need to explain. Kerra knew. She heard someone nearby murmuring, 'That was Taous. No one else can sing like that!'

Maulana was now standing up. 'Glory be to God,' he said. 'The love of God has many voices. Tonight we have had the privilege to hear one of His voices.'

Next to him Shams, an impregnable mountain of silence, was still sitting, head bent over his knees. People were looking at each other, uneasy, but their faces had softened, washed by the music, Kimya thought.

'Women, music! Maulana has lost his senses!' The man was indignant. 'And all this because of that beggar from Tabriz!'

Kimya was standing in front of a fruit stall at the edge of the market. It was early and there were still few people around. She turned her head and saw two men sitting on a cart a few steps behind her, engaged in conversation.

'You may be right, after all,' one of the men answered, the tone of his voice somewhat more restrained. 'Until now I trusted that Maulana would come back to himself, but he seems to stray further and further away from God.' The man was shaking his head in disapproval. 'That beggar has too much power over Our Master.'

Unaware of Kimya's presence, the two men continued. 'Do you know what Maulana said last night at that concert? He said that women's voices were the voice of God. What kind of nonsense is this?'

'Is that what he said?' The other man sounded shocked. 'But that is blasphemy!'

Kimya turned away. She felt sad. It was always the same. People talked and passed judgement about things they knew nothing about. For neither of these men had, of course, been at the concert. She was lost in her thoughts when she saw Hatije's mother coming towards her. Hatije's mother was a small and sturdy woman, with dark, warm eyes, always quick to give her opinion, solicited or not.

'How are you feeling today?' she asked. 'You know you fainted last night!' There was a hint of suspicion, or of slight outrage, in her voice. 'Are you taking care of yourself?'

Kimya couldn't help laughing. 'I'm taking care of myself,' she said. 'I think I was a little too hot last night, that's all.'

Hatije's mother stared at her, weighing Kimya's answer. She was not convinced. 'You're soon to be a woman,' she went on. 'Your body is growing and changing. You need to eat and sleep.' With her hands on her hips, she looked like an ancient goddess, both menacing and protective. 'You know, Kimya, I have been thinking recently, God is much simpler than men are making Him. All He wants is for us to live our life without hurting each other, and that's all.' Her eyes were bright with unshaken certainty.

Not knowing what to say, Kimya nodded in what she hoped looked like agreement. 'I must go on,' she said. 'I haven't started my shopping yet.'

'Of course, of course,' Hatije's mother approved, but she couldn't help giving a last piece of her mind. 'Music is all very well,' she said, 'but life goes on and we women have to look after our men, holy or not.'

There was an air of provocation in her eyes and Kimya wondered, What did she mean? Was she hinting that like so many others she too had reservations as to Shams's reputation and his alleged holiness?

Kimya walked away, worried and feeling powerless. She went from stall to stall, buying here a bag of peaches and there some leeks and squashes, but her heart was heavy with apprehension and attending to her shopping was an effort. Clouds were collecting above Maulana and Shams, and every day those clouds were becoming darker. How would this end?

## XVII

DAWN WAS BREAKING, SLOWLY BRINGING BACK TO LIFE THE various objects in the room: the single rose in the vase on the windowsill, the piece of embroidered silk on the wall, and next to her bed on the stool the icon of the Virgin Mary which Evdokia had given her some six years ago. Outside in the acacia tree the birds were still holding their morning meeting in a flurry of chattering, which made the silence in the house even more tangible. She took a deep breath and was going to get up when she heard footsteps outside her door, followed by Sultan Walad's voice.

'No, Father, I've not seen him.' There was an unusual note of worry in his voice.

Then she heard Kerra's: 'Perhaps he went out for an early walk.'

'This is a possibility, of course ...' Maulana's voice sounded tired and doubtful.

Kimya dressed quickly, then went straight to the kitchen where she found Kerra bent over the hearth, reviving the fire.

'You've heard,' Kerra said, turning her head towards Kimya. She didn't say more.

'Shams has gone,' Kimya said. There was no doubt in her mind about it; Shams would not be found. 'How is Maulana?' she asked.

'He went out with Sultan Walad in search of news,' Kerra said, instead of an answer.

دوست

Next to her Alim was playing with the wing feathers of the chicken they'd had for supper the previous evening. 'I'm a bird, I can fly,' he said, stretching his arms with the feathers in each hand.

Kimya laughed. 'Are you sure, Alim? You know, chickens don't fly very high.'

'I'm not a chicken!' Alim was indignant. 'I'm an eagle, and eagles fly high.'

'So they do,' she said, and for a second the image of Shams flying over Konya passed through her mind as she remembered their conversation, only a few weeks ago, when he had talked of red and green doves. And now she wondered: Had Shams flown back to Tabriz? For Shams was not a dove; he had huge wings that could spread over you and protect you, wings that could also, if he wished, take him away to the other end of the world. The memory of that conversation was so vivid that, for a second, it was as if Shams were here sitting beside her.

She gave a start when Alim, who still held the chicken feathers in his hands, came running towards her. 'You see, I can fly,' he said.

At that moment Maulana entered followed by Sultan Walad.

'Have you heard anything?' Kerra enquired.

Her husband shook his head. He looked shocked and was pale.

'Not much,' Sultan Walad said. 'No one has seen Shams. A Christian monk told us he saw a tall man walking out of the main gate early this morning before dawn. But he didn't see the man's face. It was still too dark.'

Maulana sat down heavily, two tears running down his cheeks. 'He has gone,' he murmured. 'The sun has gone.' And it was true. The house had fallen into darkness, buried under the veil of mourning.

145

دوست

Days passed. Everyone in Konya knew that Shams had left the city.

'He has gone, at last,' Maulana's students rejoiced. 'Now things will come back to normal. Now Maulana will teach us again. Soon he will forget Shams and all that madness.'

Kimya listened and again she felt like crying out: 'It's not like that at all. Maulana is in pain; he won't return to the madrassa. He won't teach you again. Don't you see, don't you feel his grief?'

Maulana now spent most of his time in his study, writing letters and poems to Shams. At times he went out to enquire whether anyone had heard about his friend. He asked the travellers, 'Have you heard about a man called Shams, Shams ud din of Tabriz? Have you seen him?'

None of them had. He begged them and some, out of pity, said that perhaps they had seen a man who looked like Shams. Then for a few hours Maulana revived until the pain overwhelmed him again. Those were the times when Kimya came and sat beside him. Sometimes she took hold of his hand and buried her cheek in its palm. Then he would smile and say, 'Kimya, oh Kimya, why has he gone?' And she thought of the roses of Tabriz and their bleeding hearts.

A few old students came to sit at the feet of their Master. He looked at them absently. Life seemed to have gone out of him.

'Maulana's house has turned into a tomb,' the students reported. 'Maulana's eyes have lost their light.'

And this was true. Happiness had deserted the house. Even little Alim muffled his voice and stopped running through the house as if afraid of the heaviness that crushed the walls, while Kerra worried because Maulana, once again, refused to eat.

146

دوست

Weeks and months elapsed. Life was as if suspended. Autumn came, then winter, until one morning Kimya woke up to an insistent bird which sent a high, cheerful note past her window. A sudden certainty came upon her: Shams will soon be back.

Later on she said to Kerra, 'Shams is getting ready. It will be only a little longer now.'

Kerra didn't question her assertion. 'Maulana will be glad,' she said simply and they looked at each other, enjoying the way women have of knowing things.

That same day a traveller from Syria knocked at the door with the news that Shams had been seen in Damascus a few weeks earlier. 'He was playing chess with a Frankish monk near the Great Mosque.' Soon a letter was sent, and from Damascus a message arrived in return. 'The rays of the sun may be obscured by clouds, but the light of the sun still illuminates the earth,' said the message. 'The rose may be hidden to the eye, yet the wind still carries its fragrance. Don't you know that whatever the heart may feel, souls never stop conversing?'

It was early morning a week later when Sultan Walad left for Syria, accompanied by a small party. The city, still held in the grip of winter, was waking up. A few people had gathered. Small clouds of mist rose from the horses' nostrils as they whinnied and kicked, impatient to depart. Standing on the threshold of the house, holding Kimya's hand, Maulana begged his son, 'Do tell him that the earth needs the warmth as well as the light of the sun.'

Sultan Walad nodded. 'I will,' he said. With his hand on his heart, he kissed his father's hand and leaped on to his horse. Soon

دوست

the small company, followed by a crowd of onlookers, was no more than a cloud of dust in the distance.

'Will he come back?' Maulana wondered aloud.

Kimya looked up at him. 'Oh, he will,' she said, as they re-entered the house. How could Maulana doubt it?

He looked at her as if suddenly discovering her after months of absence. 'You have grown up so much,' he said. He sounded surprised.

He went back to his study, leaving her alone in the semi-obscurity of the corridor. Yes, she was certain Shams would return, but, if asked, she wouldn't have been able to say whether this made her happy or not. All she could feel was a great turmoil. She ran to her room, threw herself on the bed and burst into tears. Was it relief? Was it fear? She couldn't tell.

Spring came back with its blossoms. The days started to stretch and the nights to shrink. Soon the apricots would be ready to be picked and the peaches would turn red and velvety. One morning, the news spread: Sultan Walad was on his way and Shams was with him. They would be there in a few hours' time. More than three months had gone since the small party headed by Sultan Walad had departed.

That morning Alim started to run through the house again. Outside, a crowd was gathering near the city gate and soon began to spill over the ramparts. In the kitchen Kerra and Kimya took the jar of honey and the almonds from the shelves and began preparing a pot of halwa in celebration. Then they ran out and joined the crowd that

148

دوست

awaited the travellers. Kimya looked at them and wondered at the fickleness of men. Wasn't it extraordinary? Here were not only those who had stayed loyal to the Master, but all those who had complained about Shams and his evil influence over Maulana, all those who had condemned Shams and forced him to leave. They were now revelling in his return! Had they forgotten?

She mused that almost a year ago when Shams had disappeared, she was still a child. Now she was a woman. A few months earlier, she had experienced her first menstrual pain and Kerra had rejoiced at her new womanhood. I have changed, thought Kimya. Perhaps those people have changed, too. She looked around again. The shopkeepers were there as well as the scribes and the *qadis*, the craftsmen and the students. Some of them had repented, promising that never again would they drive Shams away, that never again would they drag Maulana into despair. 'We didn't know,' they said. 'We're sorry.'

A group of musicians had gathered. They were busy settling down with their instruments. Ahead of the crowd Maulana was standing on the edge of a small escarpment overlooking the road where Sultan Walad and his companions were expected to appear. With him stood his closest friends, Salah ud din Zarkob the goldsmith, Sadruddin Qonavi whose reputation of knowledge was almost as great as Maulana's, and just behind them his faithful student Husam ud din. There was a sudden shuffling in the crowd, which parted as the Sultan Ala ud din Kaykobad and his entourage appeared mounted on horses. A palanquin soon followed with the Sultan's wife hidden behind curtains. The four men who carried the palanquin carefully placed it beside the women, assembled on one

دوست

side in an array of colours. On the hills surrounding the crowd the new grass undulated in the late morning breeze while tiny white clouds floated above the scene as if observing it. Then from the crowd a cry rose up that swelled into a roar: 'Shams is back. The sun is back!'

At the bend of the road a cloud of dust rose and horses appeared, with a group of men behind on foot. Kimya felt her heart leap, filled with the same confusing joy mingled with fear she had so often experienced since Shams's first arrival in Konya.

The man walking in front was Sultan Walad. He was holding the reins of the horse that Shams was riding. He stopped and Shams dismounted. For a second Shams stood in the midday sun staring at Maulana who seemed struck by some invisible lightning. The crowd had fallen silent. Everybody was looking at Maulana and Shams who were now walking towards each other, and then fell into each other's arms. And all of a sudden a great cry arose again from the crowd while the musicians started to play their instruments.

'It's time to go,' Kerra said, and Kimya noticed that her eyes were wet. 'Let's go and prepare the house.'

When they arrived, Ala ud din was sitting on the doorstep.

'So he has come back after all,' he said, smiling. 'Perhaps this time Father will not forget us.'

'Your father never forgot you,' Kerra said firmly. 'You should know that. But perhaps this time you will try to understand him.'

Ala ud din didn't answer; instead, he turned towards Kimya. 'And you, little sister,' he said, 'what do you make of all this? You don't look so happy, I might say.'

'Oh, Ala ud din.' Kerra sighed. 'Do you always have to tease, argue or complain?'

She suddenly sounded tired and Ala ud din blushed; then he leapt up, took Kerra's hand and kissed it. 'You're right,' he said. 'I'm not easy to live with myself.' And he ran away.

Kerra shook her head. 'This boy is unhappy and there is nothing any of us can do about it.'

# – XVIII –

T HE WAITING WAS OVER AND THE HEAVINESS THAT HAD WEIGHED
over the house ever since Shams's departure was lifted. With
his return, joy was back. Of course Maulana and Shams spent all
their time together again, but even though Kimya still missed those
evenings when Maulana would tell a story or help her read some line
in a poem, she had learned to rely more on herself and, like his grief
of the last few months, Maulana's happiness was pervasive.

She was in the kitchen stirring a vegetable stew over the fire,
thinking of Shams. He is a door, she suddenly thought, a large
door giving entry to that 'something' I can't name even when I feel
it. Every time she had had a glimpse of this 'something', it had
brought a sudden clarity and sharpness to her life, it had nourished
her and made her feel complete; it had filled her with a sense of
purpose as well as of joy and gratitude. It had found her in the
village, she reflected, and it had been waiting for her here in Konya,
like that afternoon in the snow with Hatije, or that time when she
was listening to Taous in Ana's garden. In the village the experience
had overwhelmed her, and perhaps it was that, too, that had frightened her that day when Shams had looked deep into her eyes for the
first time, throwing her into confusion.

Now she realised that this 'something' had always been a gift.
Sometimes it was like a small inner earthquake, which left her

152

دوست

panting. More often, it was like a sudden opening into a vibrant and silent world, but until now it had always come unexpectedly and as though by accident. With Shams's return all those moments were converging and his very presence allowed her almost at will to enter the place where her heart was content. Yet something had not changed: still uncomfortably woven with the very joy she felt was the thirst for more, a thirst now sharper and more painful than ever before. Am I being ungrateful? For a fleeting moment she saw Maulana smiling at her reassuringly. No you're not, he seemed to say. She looked at the large wooden spoon with which she was stirring the vegetables. Wasn't Shams stirring Konya and the household into a more fragrant dish? The thought made her smile.

'Kimya, are you dreaming?'

She started, surprised to see Kerra standing in front of her with Alim in her arms and a flicker of amusement in her eyes. Alim wriggled himself down to the floor and Kerra went to sit on the bench in the recess of the window.

'Come and sit down,' Kerra invited her, as if the family meal had all of a sudden lost its priority. Surprised, Kimya put down her spoon and, wiping her hands on a cloth, went to sit beside Kerra.

'Maulana asked me to talk to you,' Kerra began.

A wind of panic seized Kimya. Why such fear? she wondered. Was it because Kerra was so unusually solemn? I must not be afraid, she thought quickly. There is nothing to be afraid of.

Kerra was saying that since Shams's return, Maulana had been thinking how much his friend was part of their life and how much he would like this feeling to be sealed by some link, a link everybody would recognise. She heard the words without understanding them.

دوست

What did Kerra mean? The word 'wedding' hung in the air.

'What do you think, Kimya?'

She stared at Kerra, puzzled. What was she supposed to think? A wedding? 'Whose wedding?' she asked.

Kerra took her hand. 'Maulana has been thinking that you and Shams could become husband and wife,' she said. 'Is that something you would like?'

Kimya felt her body trembling. She couldn't think.

'It's a great honour, but it won't be easy,' Kerra was saying. She remained silent for a while and then added as an afterthought, 'Marriage is hard work at times, and the greater the man, the more is demanded of you.'

Kimya hid her face in her hands, overcome by a flood of emotions: terror at first, then excitement, then doubt. How could she become the wife of a man of such power as Shams! And what would it mean to be married to him? She took her hands from her face and looked at Kerra, imploring her silently for help.

'Kimya,' Kerra said, 'you have grown up here with us and —'

A loud noise interrupted her. Alim, wooden spoon in hand, was banging on the copper cauldron stored at the far corner of the room. 'See, Mama, I'm the front soldier.'

Kimya, her heart pounding in her chest, welcomed the interruption. She could hardly breathe.

'Well, Alim, that's very good,' Kerra was saying, 'but now the soldiers have arrived and they're going to have a rest.'

Alim frowned and pursed his lips. He was not sure he agreed. He banged the spoon a few more times against the cauldron and then, with a sigh, finally nodded in agreement. 'The soldiers are tired.

دوست

They're going to rest.'

'Good, and now they have to unpack and set up camp,' said Kerra. Turning back towards Kimya, she continued, 'You know, Kimya, you don't have to give your answer now. Let it all rest for a while. Like the soldiers,' she added with a laugh.

Kimya laughed too, relieved. Life had a way of inserting threads of different hues all at the same time as if to confuse you, she thought, but also to provide respite when you needed it.

'You don't even have to decide,' Kerra added. 'When the time is ripe, you'll know.' Kerra's eyes were full of little sparks and the light in them was warm and reassuring.

The wave of emotions was receding, and Kimya felt herself breathe more freely again. The doubts, the fear, and even the excitement had gone. She was left with only a great sense of calm. She closed her eyes. Kerra was right. There was nothing to decide, nothing to worry about either. All she needed to do was to listen within, as she so often forgot to do.

They sat silent, then Kerra stood up and looked at Alim sitting on the floor in a corner of the room. 'This child must be hungry; let's give him some food.'

Back at her cooking, Kimya picked a carrot out of the pot. It tasted sweet. She too was hungry, she realised. 'The stew is ready,' she said, and as she uttered the words her eyes met Kerra's and they both started to laugh, the same thought crossing their minds. Things had been stewing for a long time and now 'the stew was ready.'

'You know, Kerra,' Kimya said, 'I will marry Shams.' Strange how she now felt so calm.

'I know,' Kerra replied quietly. 'Somehow it cannot be otherwise.'

دوست

There was nothing else to say, and as if nothing had happened, the two women went on with their tasks.

'The soldiers are going to eat,' Alim announced as Kimya dipped the ladle into the pot.

On an impulse, she dropped the ladle, lifted the child in her arms and kissed him while he uttered shrill cries of excitement. 'Yes,' she said, 'the soldiers are very hungry and they're going to eat.'

Kerra's laughter was that of a young girl. 'Can I tell Maulana?' she asked.

Kimya stopped in her stride and put Alim down.

'I'm hungry, I'm very hungry,' the child complained.

Kerra was waiting.

For a second, Kimya hesitated. She could still pretend that nothing had happened. She could still be free and remain a child a little longer. She held her breath, and it was as if she were about to plunge into the coldness of a mountain stream.

'You can,' she managed to say. 'Yes, you can tell him.' There, she thought, a page has just been turned. How strange! The book of her life was being read and written, all at the same time. Wasn't it what Kerra had meant when she had said: 'You won't have to decide?' There were moments like now, when the reader and the writer were the same. She had just read a few lines in the book of her life, and her reading had been the very writing of them.

Later on, alone in her room, she realised that Kerra and she had never talked about Shams. That would have been like colluding with the gossips of Konya. They had just accepted him as one accepts the weather. Shams was a great wind that had swept through their world. The wind had come, then left, then it had returned. It could

دوست

turn itself at will into a soft breeze or a raging storm. One didn't ask the wind for reasons or justifications. One just let oneself be carried or swept away. Where would he carry her? She was still wondering when she fell asleep.

I T WAS THAT SPECIAL HOUR IN THE LATE AFTERNOON WHEN THE light caresses the world with a renewed tenderness. It was Kimya's favourite time, when everything pauses and one can reflect on the events of the day.

She was sitting in the courtyard with Hatije under the shade of the acacia tree, watching Alim watering a small rose bush with the seriousness of an apprentice gardener.

Since the announcement of her marriage the summer had gone very fast. The long nights on the roof terrace, the picking of the fruit early in the morning before the heat forced everyone indoors, the slow walks in Qamar al din Garden after the evening prayer; all this was almost over. Already the air carried a new coolness and the leaves on the trees had that tired look announcing the approach of autumn. As in her life, she thought, everything was subtly changing colour, making itself ready for the next turn of events.

The early comments about her forthcoming marriage had slowly faded. Some said that such a marriage was a good thing, that it would make Shams more approachable, more like everybody else. But some women had asked what kind of a husband Shams would be. 'Men like him don't get tamed,' they had remarked, shaking their heads knowingly. Then after a while the women had turned to other concerns. What would Kimya wear for the wedding? Would

158

there be many guests? Who was to prepare the food?

Curiously Hatije had kept very quiet. 'Aren't you afraid?' she once asked, and Kimya tried to explain – more to herself than to Hatije – that, yes, she was afraid but she had no doubt about her decision.

'I'm just following what is already written.'

Hatije had stared at her with her usual incomprehension. 'So it's not really your decision,' she remarked.

Kimya replied that, on the contrary, to agree to marry Shams was very much her own decision. 'Because, you see, we can either refuse or accept what is offered, but the only thing that matters is to know whether it is written or not. Once you know, it's better to accept and let life take over. Then everything may look the same, but it feels completely different.'

'Then are you happy?' Hatije asked.

The question took Kimya by surprise. It was not something she ever asked herself. 'I don't know.' Was happiness the only yardstick with which to measure one's life? She was not sure. 'There are moments when I feel sad,' Kimya admitted. 'Life keeps changing and one cannot go back.'

She remembered a warning from Maulana, a few years earlier. They were sitting in his study together, bent over a book of poetry. The poem they were reading talked of a stream running down the mountain. It had revived memories of her life in the village, and with them had surged up a sadness and a longing for what was past. Maulana had taken her chin in his hand and looked into her eyes.

'I know, Kimya. Nostalgia is a powerful and cunning witch. If you are not careful, she will seduce you back into the past and suck the sap out of your life. Then you'll find yourself empty-handed with only misty dreams for comfort.'

She had shivered at the vision of a witch trying to grasp her in her claws.

Maulana had continued, 'You see, Kimya, the Great Sustainer is here in front of you, at this very minute. If you are busy looking back, or into the future for that matter, you are not seeing Him; you are forgetting Him. And if you forget Him' –Maulana had shaken his head – 'then life is not worth living.'

It was so simple, and yet so difficult not to let oneself be caught by the desire to stop life in its course. She shook herself out of her mood. Hatije was watching her, her curiosity mixed with concern.

Kimya jumped to her feet. 'Hatije, don't worry. You asked me whether I was afraid, but to be afraid or sad doesn't mean one is making a mistake. It just means one is not listening carefully enough.'

'Oh, Kimya, you make me mad,' Hatije cried out. 'I don't understand a word of what you say. Sometimes I think you don't know anything about life.' She was shaking her fists in a gesture of frustration. 'And sometimes I think I am the one who knows nothing.'

Kimya laughed. 'We both know nothing. There is so much to learn! But what I do know is that you make me laugh and that I love you.' And taking Alim in her arms, she turned on her heels while the child shrieked with delight.

# – XX –

SADRUDDIN QONAVI STANDS FACING HER. AS SO OFTEN IN other times, Maulana's old friend is acting as leader of the prayer, and today it is for her wedding. Next to her, like a tall, silent mountain, stands the man whose eyes once made her soul shiver, the man to whom Maulana has given his heart, Shams, her husband soon to be.

She is wearing an orange kaftan, embroidered at the neck and wrists with golden thread. Her hair, parted down the middle, is covered with a veil of white muslin fixed in place by a small diadem of silver and pearls – Kerra's present to her. The veil, sewn with the traditional thread of seven colours, hides her face so that she can see without being exposed to the curiosity of the people present. She is vaguely aware of the scent of musk which Kerra has rubbed over her neck and wrists. It's strange to feel so calm now after the agitation of the last weeks, busy as they were with the preparations for the wedding: the food, her dress, the list of guests. Few people have been invited, though: only Maulana's closest friends and her own close friends such as Hatije and Nuran, with their families.

The room, ablaze with candles, is fragrant with the scent of the roses and jasmine that decorate the walls. Above the flickering flames the air is trembling as if turned liquid and through her veil the whole scene has an unreal quality. Curiously, she feels more like a guest look-

161

دوست

ing from afar at her wedding than the bride attending it.

Maulana is sitting a few steps away from Sadruddin. In the blue-green of his eyes, the light shines more brightly than usual. Standing behind him and Sadruddin are Sultan Walad, Ala ud din, and some of their friends, all looking solemn, plus some older men Kimya has seen at times in Maulana's study. On the other side of the room, slightly apart, the wives and young women are sitting on the cushions laid out there for the occasion. In contrast with the cheerful faces of the women surrounding her, Kerra, sitting very straight, wears a severe expression on her face. What can she be thinking? To the dismay of many a citizen of Konya, this is, of course, a most unusual wedding where Christian and Muslim customs are strangely inter-woven. Could it be that Kerra deplores that the strict custom of total separation between bride and groom has been overlooked today? Does she perhaps regret that this bride will not go and live with the family of her new husband, since Shams has no home of his own, and no family either? Kimya pushes the absurd thoughts away. She hears Sadruddin's voice addressing Shams.

'Do you accept Kimya, the daughter of Maulana, Our Master Jalal ud din of Rum, as your faithful wife?'

There is a pause, then Shams's voice rises, hoarse in the silence. 'I do accept Kimya, the daughter of Maulana, Jalal ud din of Rum, as my faithful wife.'

Sadruddin is now turning towards her. 'Do you accept Shams ud din of Tabriz as your devoted husband?'

Time stops for a moment. The imam is waiting.

'I do accept Shams ud din of Tabriz as my devoted husband.' Her voice is firm in spite of her heart, which seems to want to escape from her chest.

162

'You are now husband and wife,' Sadruddin pronounces.

She lifts her veil and, to her amazement, Shams takes her hands. The silence in the room has become palpable. Doesn't he know that couples are never supposed to touch in public? Their eyes meet. But what she sees is so unexpected that her mind goes blank. There in front of her, this tall, powerful man is looking shy and embarrassed and, even more unexpected, there is something resembling admiration in his eyes. And now he raises her hands and, bending towards her, brushes them with his lips. There is a silent gasp in the room. She feels herself blushing, though not for herself, but for him, so exposed, so vulnerable. So this is how it feels to be a woman! She smiles, a light smile for all present to see. Only she doesn't know she is smiling.

The day seems to stretch endlessly. The men have left the room to gather in Maulana's study with the musicians specially hired for the occasion. One can hear them talking and laughing over the sound of the *ney* and the *rebab*, with the beat of the drum in the background. Kimya now sits with Kerra's friends and her own friends, Hatije beside her. Here too, the room is full of talk and laughter. She is sitting on a pile of cushions, slightly higher than the rest of the women so that she doesn't forget that she is the bride and must stand out today. In front of her on the white cloth spread in the direction of Mecca rests the mirror of happiness given by Shams, with the two candles still burning on each side of it: one for Shams, one for her.

'Fire and the reflection of fire!' Sadruddin al Qonavi had murmured when Maulana had lit them at the beginning of the ceremony.

163

دوست

'Look how the flames are waving,' a woman exclaims. 'How can this be? There is no wind here!'

'Well, this is Shams's mirror!' another woman comments, implying, 'What do you expect if not the unexpected?' And now the two women are looking at Kimya with an air of commiseration.

Will this day never end? More dishes are being brought. The candles are dripping.

'You're not eating, Kimya. Try this, it's delicious.' The woman is offering Kimya a piece of halwa. 'You're a married woman now,' she says, 'and soon you will have children.'

Kimya takes the halwa. She doesn't know what to say. She notices Hatije's mother coming towards her.

'Marriage may feel strange at first,' Hatije's mother says as she sits down and makes herself comfortable, 'but you will get used to it. Of course, men are sometimes difficult to please ...'

'Mama, today is a day of joy and celebration!'

'I know, I know, Hatije, but still there is no harm in telling things the way they are.'

Kimya hears the words; she even understands each one of them, yet together they have no meaning. She sees Hatije's mother, her sturdiness, her cheeks aflame, and she wants to say: 'Look, it doesn't matter what men are or are not. Today I have married both the raging wind and the soft breeze. Today I have married the lion's roar and the tender foal.' A sudden silence has fallen upon the room, engulfing the sound of the women's voices. In front of her the flames of the two candles have stopped moving. She wants to cry out: 'Today I have entered fire and it feels like frozen snow.' But the words remain locked in her throat, as part of the secret pact she has

دوست

just entered. She shuts her eyes and is startled when, as suddenly as all sound had vanished, the brouhaha of the women's voices returns and in the background the low voices of the men and the sound of the flute over the drum. The flames of the two candles are dancing again in front of her and there is a strange taste of salt in her mouth. She presses her handkerchief to her lips and finds on it a small stain of blood. She must have bitten her lips.

'Kimya, you're shivering. Here, put this shawl around you and have some tea.'

Kerra is facing her, her eyes saying, 'Steady, I am here, everything is all right.'

She takes a few sips and shuts her eyes again. A wave of gratitude overtakes her. 'Oh, God, once again, you are giving me so much!' Then, to Kerra's obvious relief, she starts to laugh, because she has no idea what she is thankful for and yet the feeling of gratitude makes her heart sing. Gratitude is a gift, too! she realises. It multiplies a hundred times the desire to thank. It's like becoming aware of the coolness of the breeze in the middle of summer, or of the warmth of the log fire in the middle of winter. It makes each cell long to sing.

They have walked slowly to the south-east wing of the house where, until recently, Shams had his lodging. It consists of three rooms and connects with the rest of the house through a door leading to a small courtyard. Opposite that door is another door that leads directly to the street. Over the last few weeks the whole place has been converted into new lodgings for the two of them. When the guests had left and the music finally come to an end, Maulana had kissed her

165

دوست

on the forehead before retiring. Kerra, too, had kissed her brow and then stroked her cheek.

Now the silence between her and Shams is like the veil she wore on her head a few hours earlier. Then it protected not only her; it protected them both. And now the veil of silence says: 'Wait a little, slow down, let this moment last for ever.'

In front of the door, dozens of small, yellow roses have been spread out on the ground as a sign of welcome. As they walk in, the fragrance surrounds them. The thought crosses her mind that she has just crossed a new threshold, entered the unknown territory of her new life. They are now standing face to face in the hallway. It is her turn to feel shy. Then, once again, he takes her hands and brings them to his lips. This time it feels like a seal, the seal of their new life together. It must have all been planned in that other place that is no place at all, that place where time stops and where she, herself, is no more. He looks at her as if waiting for her to say something. But what can she say? He nods as if he understands and indicates a door on her left. 'You must be tired; here is your room. Sleep in peace and remember: He is with you, always.' He hands her the candle he is carrying, and brusquely turns away and disappears into his room.

She is alone in the hallway, her shadow stretching along the wall. Slowly she goes towards the room he has indicated and pushes open the door. It is a small room, similar to the one she occupied in the other part of the house. Flickering in the dark, the flame of an oil lamp placed on a stool next to the bed sends ripples of light on the geometric patterns of a rug woven in hues of saffron and dark red. All at once she notices on the bed a small yellow rose like the ones carpeting the entrance. She takes the flower in her hands. Its yellow petals have a touch of red on them, like her handkerchief with the bloodstain on it. A rose stained with blood! Like the roses of Tabriz Shams had once mentioned! She shivers and quickly undresses. She lies awake for a while and then, as she drifts into sleep, the words form themselves on her lips: 'I am with you, always.' Who is saying the words? She is not sure.

She woke up with the morning call to prayer. Next to her was a wall she didn't remember. Where was she? Then it all came back: the wedding, her wedding, Shams kissing her hands and herself alone in the hallway with the candle flickering in her hand. She had slept soundly. I'm married, she said to herself, wondering what this new status required of her. Then she heard Shams's heavy footsteps outside, followed by the moaning of the front door. She visualised the courtyard with its small fountain, now part of their private quarters. She had often come here, sometimes in the early hours of the morning, sometimes in the afternoon, to prepare a tray of refreshments, using the same cooking area where she now began to make the morning tea. Someone – could it be Shams? – had put embers in the hearth. She reflected that life didn't seem to have changed much since the previous day. Was she relieved or disappointed? She started to sing softly to herself as she often did when she was uncertain about her feelings.

'You're wise to suspend your questions, Kimya.'

The voice startled her. He was standing in the doorway, looking half serious, half amused. She felt slightly annoyed. How was she to live with someone who always read her mind?

167

دوست

He apparently ignored that last thought of hers. 'Change comes from within, not from outside. Don't you know that?'

She nodded, glad that there was no reproach in his voice. She looked at him but could read nothing on his face.

'Shall I bring your tea to your room?' she asked.

'That would be good,' he said, then he added, 'Don't let expectations distort reality. You would be wasting a very precious time.'

This time there was a faint smile on his lips, but his eyes were sharp, and each one of his words had the precision of an arrow carefully aimed at its goal. Curiously she could feel their impact, yet without really knowing what to make of them.

'Your singing is the answer,' he said, as if once again he were answering her unspoken question. 'Singing is one of the ways the soul makes itself heard.'

He turned away as if he had already said too much and walked back to his room.

She finished preparing the tray: a bowl of black olives, a few pieces of cheese, and finally the jug of hot tea. Then on an impulse she went to fetch the small rose in her room and placed it next to the jug. Her heart was pounding. She laughed to herself. Joy, she thought, must be another way our souls talk to us.

WINTER WAS OVER, YET SPRING WAS HARDLY HERE. KIMYA had decided to sit in the courtyard and was enjoying the early afternoon sun though it was not quite warm enough to stay there long. It was now more than three moons since her wedding, she reflected. As she did every morning after prayer, she had prepared Shams's early meal: the bowl of black olives, the squares of white goat's cheese, the jug of hot tea. As on most mornings Shams was already gone when she got up – she had heard his footsteps earlier. But sometimes he came back and then he wanted some food. She thought that, apart from that early morning task, her life had hardly changed. She still went to the market with Kerra. She still helped her with the various tasks of the house. She still looked after Alim from time to time, and still took trays of food and refreshments to Maulana's study, where he and Shams remained shut in together for most of the day.

It was only in the way people related to her that she felt a subtle change had taken place, at least in their eyes. It was as if the veil of her wedding had not been removed from her head. To them she was not Kimya any more but a married woman; that is, a remote abstraction which demanded a certain kind of behaviour. She remembered Hatije's mother saying, 'It will feel strange at first, but you will get used to it.' Get used to no longer running for just the pleasure of it!

169

دوست

Get used to no longer laughing too loudly in public! 'Married women must show poise and restraint,' she had been told, 'and they must please their husbands.' But how was she to please her husband when she hardly ever saw him? And would it please Shams if she stopped being herself? Yet she wondered: What was this joy she felt every morning when preparing that first meal of his? She sighed. There were so many questions she couldn't answer! Previously, she would have discussed all this with Hatije or even Nuran who held strong opinions about the world and how it should be. But now there was an invisible barrier between her and her friends. For how could she tell them of the strange intimacy she shared with Shams? How could she speak of a non-existent married life which, however lonely she felt at times, was also filling her with joy? And anyhow that joy was too fragile. Once exposed, it would vanish as surely as footprints blown away by the wind.

The bench on which she was sitting felt cold suddenly in spite of the sun. Over the wall the cherry tree, its branches still naked, seemed to be begging the sky for more warmth. She let her mind drift again over the past few months. She could still see Hatije, close to tears and complaining, 'We are not really talking to each other any more.' She had nodded, sadly aware that their conversations had lost their previous spontaneity and become superficial. Since that day Hatije's visits had shortened, then become scarce.

Her relationship with Kerra had also changed, though in a different way. Kerra never asked questions. She didn't need to, any more than she needed to explain herself. Without a word Kerra subtly indicated that Kimya was now on her own, that the reassurance and safeguarding Kerra had offered all these years were not as

170

دوست

readily available any more. It was for Kimya to find in herself the reassurance and protection she needed. Kerra was not going to intrude into Kimya's new life, just as she never intruded into Maulana's when it came to his relationship with Shams. Kimya remembered the evening of her wedding when she and Shams had stepped into their new lodgings. She had entered a new territory then, and in this new territory there was no one but Shams and herself.

The rattling of a cart and the clip-clop of a horse beyond the wall distracted her for a moment. Strange how the world outside felt more and more remote! There were days like today when she felt abandoned. And yet there was the joy! How could she feel joy and almost at the same time feel utterly lost, belonging nowhere? Did growing up entail facing more and more contradictions? When she lived in the village there had been no one to confide in, and yet there had been moments then when she dissolved in joy, losing all sense of time and space, only to burst into tears afterwards because the joy had vanished. Here in Maulana's house the loneliness had receded. She had found herself more at home with her adopted family than with her own parents, nourished in a way she couldn't explain, but now the loneliness was back. Would this loneliness with its accompanying longing ever leave her? During the last few weeks she had tried to keep herself busy with extra visits to the market, but once in front of the stalls she couldn't remember what it was she wanted. She had gone to a small church on the outskirts of the bazaar and knelt at the feet of the Virgin, but she had found no nourishment there and left feeling empty and sad. She had tried again to talk with Hatije, but once more it had ended in disappointment. I am

171

like a ball bouncing back off a blank wall, she thought, staring at the wall in front of her where a tiny plant was attempting to grow with not enough soil for it to take root.

She shivered and pulled her shawl around her shoulders. Married women spend time with their husbands, she thought. But Shams was hardly ever around. There were times like this morning, before dawn and the call to prayer, when all she heard were his footsteps followed by the screech of the bolt and the creaking of the door. Then the day dragged on endlessly, until she heard his steps again late in the night. The first time, she had come to the door to welcome him, but he had ignored her and gone straight to his room grumbling, 'Do not bother. Go to sleep. It's late.'

Perplexed, she had watched him disappear into his room. What was she supposed to do? What was a married woman supposed to do? That night, unable to find sleep, she had heard him walking about in his room, murmuring words she could not catch. Later, in the early hours when she woke up, he was gone.

She looked around. The cherry tree was in bud after all. Funny how it had escaped her! Would it have pink or white blossoms? she wondered. Her thoughts went back to Shams. Would he return earlier, as he sometimes did? She never knew. There had been days when he had come back unexpectedly at midday or in the afternoon, asking for a piece of cheese or a glass of tea and then retiring to his room.

At that moment she heard the door from the main house opening. There he was, looking at her. She stood up, as if caught at fault. It was still morning, and Shams had never come back so early. The shadow of a smile fluttered on his lips. He walked slowly towards

دوست

the bench and sat down, ignoring her embarrassment.

'Why don't you bring us some tea?' he said.

She had never heard him say 'us' before. This was new and soothing, a balm on the wound of her loneliness. She went to prepare the tea and was soon back in the courtyard with the tray. She had started to fill his glass when he looked deep into her eyes. As so often, his face was stern and impersonal. She could tell he was not looking at her in the way a man looks at a woman, or even a friend at a friend. No, he was looking somewhere beyond, into that place of silence where joy was waiting, where words she knew nothing of were ready to come to her lips. She saw her hand trembling and the tea spilling. His eyes softened, then, to her surprise, he started to laugh, that deep laughter of his that was like the rumble of thunder.

'Kimya, why do you worry? Why be frightened? I know it is hard to keep your feet on the earth while your heart looks for the heavens. But the secret is' – he paused, now almost smiling – 'the secret is that the earth and the heavens are not apart.' He brought the glass of tea to his lips. 'Not at all apart,' he repeated, his face serious again.

She remained standing in front of him, trying to hold on to his words. But already they had slipped from her mind and all she could remember was his question: 'Why do you worry?' Why did she indeed? Shams had shut his eyes, as if saying: 'Let it all rest. I won't hold you with my gaze. You are free now.' She was still standing in front of him when he opened his eyes.

'I must go now,' he said, and soon he disappeared through the same door he had come in.

دوست

What had made him come? She had no idea.

A few days later she was sitting on the bench in the courtyard again, facing the door to the main house and half expecting to see Shams appear through it. But of course he would not. Things never repeat themselves. They were not meant to. At least the weather had not changed. It was still not quite warm enough to sit outside for very long. Her thoughts went back to those moments with Shams, so short, so few, but like sparks in the night. She sighed. There was no one she could talk to about it. A faint sound, like the rustling of leaves, made her look towards the door in front of her. For a split second, her heart leaped in hope and fear. But it was Ala ud din who stood in the doorway. His eyes were fixed on her. How long had he been there? He looked sad and angry. And as so often with Ala ud din, she felt ill at ease. He always seemed to carry a heavy burden. You wanted to help him, you wanted to make him smile, but his stubborn self-pity wouldn't let you come near. She forced a smile. 'I didn't hear you coming.' Then, as he didn't reply, she added, 'Shams is not here.'

Ala ud din still said nothing.

'Would you like to wait for him? He might come back. Sometimes he does in the morning.'

'I see.' He stayed there, swaying awkwardly on his feet, still staring at her. 'I see.' He then turned back and was gone.

What did he mean? She had pretended to believe he was looking for Shams, but she knew he was not. He probably doesn't know himself why he has come, she thought. Ala ud din often acted on an impulse; that's how he was. Still, his visit left her feeling uncomfortable. Should she tell Shams? But what could she tell him? There was

174

دوست

nothing to say.

Three days later, as she was opening the door to the main part of the house, Ala ud din was there again, blocking the entrance.

'Ala ud din, let me pass. Kerra is waiting for me.' She was angry.

'You were not so proud before. Marriage has gone to your head,' he said, making just enough room for her to pass through so that her kaftan rubbed against his when she went in.

She shrugged. 'You are being ridiculous. Why don't you leave me alone?' She was becoming upset. Ala ud din had always been difficult, teasing her or pointing out her mistakes when she spoke Persian, but it had always been in front of Kerra or Sultan Walad who, after a while, made him stop. This time, however, it was just the two of them and she didn't like the curious complicity he had managed to establish between them by forcing his presence upon her. She walked faster than usual down the corridor leading to the large kitchen where Kerra was expecting her. She was aware of Ala ud din walking a few steps behind, but before she reached the kitchen he had turned towards the main courtyard. She stopped for a second and watched him disappear through the front gate. She found herself left with an unpleasant taste in her mouth.

It was a glorious evening. The sky was of such a deep blue it felt almost solid. Reaching over the wall from the street the white blossoms of the cherry tree – they were white, after all – seemed to be heralding the spring. The walls lit by the sun were aflame. Shams had left early at dawn as usual, but today he had returned before nightfall, just a few minutes ago.

'I want to show you something,' he said, and went to his room

دوست

while she busied herself making the tea she had prepared earlier.

The door of their lodgings was still open to the courtyard, allowing a ray of gold to reach her feet. She was singing to herself, thinking that they would go and sit on the old stone bench outside, when she heard the door to the main part of the house opening. She looked up. As before, Ala ud din was standing in the doorway. At that moment, Shams came out of his room. He noticed Kimya was startled and then caught sight of Ala ud din.

The two men stared at each other, each of them surprised to see the other. After a few seconds, Ala ud din, having recovered his composure, started to walk in the direction of the door leading to the street.

'And where do you think you're going, Ala ud din?' asked Shams.

'I'm going to the bazaar,' Ala ud din replied defiantly. 'Father needs a quill and some paper, and I have heard of a shipment of parchment newly arrived from Syria.'

There was a silence. Behind Shams Kimya had not moved.

'And the best way to the bazaar is through this courtyard!' Shams said. The sarcasm in his voice was worse than a reproach.

The youth remained silent, visibly ill at ease and in a hurry to escape from Shams's glare.

But Shams had not finished. 'This is private now,' he reminded Ala ud din, 'and you know it. It's not a place for you to come to or walk through unless invited.'

Ala ud din's face had turned red. His jaws were tight. But the glare in Shams's eyes kept him subdued. He couldn't help muttering however, 'As it happens, this is also my father's house.'

'Ala ud din, don't provoke me.' Shams's voice had become

menacing. 'Your father, as you perfectly well know, would not approve. And you also know that this door to the street is kept locked.'

Momentarily defeated, Ala ud din lowered his head and, turning back, walked brusquely to the door of the main house and disappeared.

Shams shook his head. 'So much anger in this boy!' He turned towards Kimya. 'Now he won't trouble you any more,' he said, implying that he knew this was not the first time Ala ud din had come to this part of the house. 'Young cubs may have sharp teeth,' he went on, 'but they have no power and they know it.' He laughed. 'Sometimes that makes them angry.' She noticed that the line between his eyebrows had disappeared.

'Let's have this tea,' he said, indicating that Ala ud din's intrusion was not worth more attention. 'Look.' He was holding a piece of parchment in his hand. 'This is what I wanted to show you.'

It was a small painting of a bird with the face of a woman gazing towards the left. The body of the bird was of a deep blue, while the face, calm, inward-looking, yet acutely attentive, was drawn in black lines. Swimming around, and the same deep blue as the bird, were two fish, suggesting that here was a reality where space and time had lost their boundaries. The painting's strange and vivid beauty was like a door to another world, close, yet unreachable.

Kimya's eyes filled with tears. She handed the picture back to Shams, unable to speak.

'Yes,' he said. 'It's very beautiful.' He paused. 'Like you,' he added.

She stared at him, taken aback. Was he making fun of her?

دوست

But there was no trace of irony or mockery in his eyes, just a slight embarrassment which he tried to hide behind a stern face. It reminded her of the day of their wedding. She felt her cheeks burning and hid her own embarrassment by drinking her tea.

The courtyard was slowly sinking into darkness. Only the patch of white blossoms on the left marked its limits. The thought crossed her mind that soon the cherry tree would exchange its white blossoms for a more sober garb of green. Shams had closed his eyes, and she was wondering if he were still aware of her presence when, without opening his eyes, he said, 'Do sit down.' She obeyed, aware of the power suddenly filling the whole courtyard. As she sat there beside Shams, a wave of overwhelming joy submerged her, then she heard him say, 'I am going now. I'll see you some time later or tomorrow.'

He was standing in front of her, his face as inscrutable as ever and she nodded, unable to speak or to move.

'You'll be all right,' he said. Then he was gone.

# – XXII –

SHE WAS LYING IN BED WIDE AWAKE. SHAMS HAD BEEN AWAY all day, and now the night was far advanced and he still had not returned. She wondered why they were married. Did being married mean living together like brother and sister, or rather like father and daughter? Did being married mean hardly ever seeing each other? Yet when Shams was around, she felt sustained, satisfied. His presence somehow readjusted reality, sharpened it. It enlarged her world, making the worries and concerns of daily life look like small ripples on the surface of a lake. Then she was able to remember it was the lake that mattered, not the ripples; and that in this expanded reality she had her own unique place – small, no doubt, but purposeful.

She was surprised at herself. Her feelings towards Shams had changed over the last few months. His power and his authority still overwhelmed her, but her fear of him had diminished. She now knew that other side of him, which she had first witnessed on the day of their wedding, that mixture of shyness and tenderness that he couldn't completely hide when they were together. To discover such vulnerability in a man of such power had astonished her at first, but also moved her. Paradoxically his very vulnerability made him even greater. Shams was not – at least not only – the superhuman being everyone feared. He was also someone life could hurt.

دوست

She shut her eyes, overcome by this thought. Then she was standing on a vast plain of sand and rocks, alone in a brown, reddish landscape, a white sun hovering over the horizon in a sky made of liquid waves. And there, at the junction between sky and earth, something started to move – a shape, the shape of a beast that seemed to be walking towards her. As it approached, she saw it was a gigantic lion. It walked smoothly, with a kind of determination, clearly aware of her presence. She could see its mane, tangled and unkempt, and its muscles moving under the skin. In terror, she tried to flee, only to find herself glued to the ground. The lion was now so close that she could feel its breath. Then, to her utter amazement, it lay down at her feet and licked her hand.

She woke, with the taste of terror mixed with sweetness, relieved to find she was in bed. The rasping of the bolt followed by the sound of Shams's footsteps had somehow become part of the dream, if indeed it was a dream. Under her door a ray of light shone for a few seconds and then vanished, as if engulfed by the silence, and she let herself fall back into the dark sweetness of her dream.

She was in bed the following night, after a similar day of solitude, when she became aware of a crackling sound in the house, like the sound of fire in the hearth when the wood bursts open from the heat. Under her door was a bright glow. She jumped out of bed and rushed out of her room. The door of Shams's room was open and it was there that the fire was roaring. She approached, horrified – then incredulous. Inside, surrounded by flames and with his eyes closed, Shams was sitting unconcerned. His face, colourless, seemed carved in stone. Her first impulse was to run inside and help him out, but something about the scene held her back. The flames were rising and falling without touching him, more like a protection than a threat. Aghast, she remained there gazing at him encircled by fire, until she retreated shivering to her room. Only then did she realise that the flames she had just witnessed didn't produce any heat. She lay awake for a long time, her mind in turmoil.

The call to prayer woke her up. She must have slept only a few minutes, or so it seemed. The images of the night surged back, the circle of flames around Shams, his ashen face. Had it all been a dream? She dressed quickly and opened the door. Shams was coming out of his room, with an oil lamp in his hand. He seemed surprised to see her there, as if he had forgotten that they were sharing the same lodgings. She noticed the dark marks under his eyes; but the spark in them was brighter than ever. He stopped for a second, then said, 'Never be afraid. His fire is like water to the garden.'

The words were balm on some invisible wound. So it had not been a dream!

'It is that fire that you must seek,' he added, before entering the courtyard to go to the fountain for his morning ablutions. She stayed in the doorway, watching him going through the ritual. He dried his hands and had already reached the door to the main house when he turned back: 'What you saw last night, was a gift of His. It is not to be talked about.'

She nodded, disappointed that he had felt it necessary to warn her. Didn't he know that her lips were sealed when it came to their life together, this mixture of loneliness and precious moments? But he had disappeared and again she was alone. In the white coldness of dawn that was slowly erasing the night the fountain was now clearly visible.

دوست

The sun had been battering the walls of the courtyard all afternoon. On the other side of the wall the cherry tree had finally lost its blossoms to its new robe of green. Summer was approaching. Kimya was sitting on the old stone bench, her hands busy with a tiny crochet hook and a roll of white cotton thread. Funny how she had lost her appetite for reading recently, attracted instead to more manual tasks like this lace making which brought back memories of her sister and her life in the village. Those memories had grown blurred with the years, but the emotion attached to them was still there: her joy at Father Chrisostom teaching her the Greek letters; her excitement when, for the first time, she had seen the Persian word *doost* which Ahmed had written in the dust. How amazing to discover years later that all along, though unknown to her, the way was already mapped.

She brushed the memories away and returned to the present. It was hot and she was feeling sleepy. She bent down to retrieve the crochet hook that had fallen at her feet and her thoughts turned to Shams. He had come back earlier, only to leave again soon afterwards. As so often he had refused the food she had prepared, though she knew he had eaten nothing since the previous night. He had mentioned an invitation to an evening organised by Sadruddin Qonavi. But would he actually eat any of the meal that was certain to be part of the evening? She doubted it. She reflected that living with Shams was unsettling. There were no points of reference, no clear, obvious rhythm. At times Shams even ignored the call to prayer, yet at night when he was at home, she could hear him repeating the names of God. How was she to pray? How was she supposed to live her life? A recent visit by Nuran had not helped.

دوست

'People believe that Shams is making you dreadfully unhappy,' Nuran had confessed. 'You don't go out as often as before and they say it's because he is so furiously jealous that he forbids you.'

Kimya had shaken her head in disbelief. How can people be so stupid! She was shocked.

But Nuran wouldn't stop. 'And what of his ways! Shams hardly ever goes to the mosque and it is known that he once drank wine.'

At that point, Kimya had silenced her. 'That is gossip. People have no idea of who he is. And, Nuran, you should remember that, though I am your friend, Shams is my husband.'

Nuran had left looking sheepish but also angry.

People may believe what they want, Kimya now reflected. Shams knows what he is doing and why he is doing it. He never acted on a whim or an impulse; of that she was sure. Instead he followed an inner order as natural to him as breathing, waking or falling asleep. This of course didn't always agree with people's habits or conventions. But such was his freedom! She herself had had a taste of this freedom that day she had agreed to marry Shams. She had not willed it then, nor had she responded to any outside pressure. She had simply been allowed to see that marrying Shams was already written, that it was in the order of things. How strange! Freedom was only to obey that order of things. But to be as free as Shams all the time requires a strength I do not possess, she thought.

The sound of the door on her left interrupted her thoughts. It was Kerra holding Alim by the hand. She was smiling and looked younger than usual.

'Yes, Alim, Kimya is here. Can we come in?'

'Of course. Do come in and sit with me.'

دوست

The child ran towards her and buried his head in her kaftan. She stroked him, pleased to be distracted from her thoughts.

'He was asking for you. How could I resist him?'

'You couldn't,' said Kimya, laughing. 'No one can resist Alim, can they?' She ruffled the boy's hair and the child looked up at her with laughter in his eyes. He showed her a handful of nuts.

'I see, you brought some nuts. Why don't you go and play with them?'

Apparently satisfied, Alim sat down on the ground and applied himself to making one of the nuts spin on itself. This was a familiar game. Children kept hazelnuts and for hours competed at making them spin. Kimya remembered how, to her disappointment, her nuts had always ended up turning unevenly and finally stopped.

Kerra sat beside her. They listened to the twittering of the birds. 'They are busy building their nests,' Kerra remarked.

Kimya nodded. 'They are lucky. They always know exactly what to do, don't they?'

'You mean you don't always know what to do!' Kerra was laughing, obviously mocking her. 'But, Kimya, that is our privilege as human beings.'

Privilege! What privilege was there in stumbling through life, most of the time not knowing what to do?

Kerra was looking at her, amused. 'To be human is like walking on a tightrope. This is the privilege. I agree it's difficult, but this is how we learn.'

'But how?' Kimya exclaimed. 'Sometimes I know, and sometimes I don't.'

'This is what I mean. We are more than birds, but we are not

184

دوست

angels – not yet at least.' The look of amusement in her eyes was still there. 'It's uncomfortable, I must admit, but yes, it is our privilege,' she repeated. She grew serious. 'Look at him,' she said, indicating her young son playing with the hazelnuts. 'He's so full of trust.' She paused and something like the shadow of a smile fluttered on her face. 'We need to become transparent,' she finally said, 'so that we can hear Him whispering. This is what trust is.'

'This is how Shams and Maulana live,' Kimya murmured, 'isn't it?'

Kerra nodded. 'There is no other way. Once the fears, the likes and dislikes, the doubts have dropped, then nothing interferes any more, and He can be heard.'

That great calm emanating from Kerra, so light, so warm, so immensely soothing! thought Kimya.

Kerra shook her head. 'Sometimes we are simply too impatient, and today' – the smile in her eyes had reappeared – 'today, both of us are also much too serious.' As if answering her, a bird started to sing somewhere in the cherry tree. They looked at each other and began to laugh. 'Yes,' Kerra said, 'the birds never forget to give thanks.'

At their feet, Alim was clapping. 'Look, look. It's spinning.' One of the nuts was turning as though caught in a miniature tornado.

'Oh, Alim! You're so clever!' Kimya cried out.

The child sat up, beaming with pride. 'These are good nuts,' he said. 'Sultan Walad gave them to me.'

'Well, if Sultan Walad gave them to you,' Kerra said, 'they must be good nuts.'

# – XXIII –

SHE WOKE SUDDENLY, HER BODY SOAKED IN PERSPIRATION. For a second she thought it was night. But the ray of sun that crossed her bed told her it was the middle of the afternoon, one of those summer afternoons when the heat beats you into a heavy sleep. Even the silence was dense, with no sound of birds chirping and twittering. She remembered that Shams had left in the early hours of the morning. After sweeping his room and hers as well as the courtyard, she had eaten a few pieces of cheese and bread left over from the previous day, tried to read a book of poetry by Sanai, and finally fallen asleep. She felt drowsy and decided to go out into the courtyard. At least there would be some air outside.

The light blinded her as she walked into the open. The sun was still high and the heat was more intense here than inside the house, yet the sound of the fountain made it somehow more bearable. She plunged her arms into the water with relief. The coolness of the evening was still some hours away and she wondered: Would there be music tonight on the roof terrace? Or like the previous night, only the burning presence of Shams and Maulana? She longed for those evenings far more than for their relative coolness.

She felt lonely today, abandoned. Though her heart might well be always with Shams, that was not enough to fill her solitude. And the loneliness was even more difficult to bear these days

186

دوست

because of those strange moments when, in the most incomprehensible way, she found herself in Maulana's study with Shams, though she remained where she was, sitting quietly on her bed or engaged in some manual task somewhere else. Once, as she was again mysteriously transported into Maulana's study with Shams, who stared at her with a faint smile on his face, she looked down at her hands resting on her lap but, to her amazement, there was nothing there to see except the embroidered cushion on which she was sitting. She, or rather her body, was not there! Alarmed, she stood up and went to gaze into the small round mirror that hung on one of the walls, only to find that there was no reflection!

'Where have I gone?' she exclaimed.

'There is no need for a candle when you are in front of the sun. Is there?' Maulana had remarked casually. 'You shouldn't be surprised.'

Shams, who sat facing them, had nodded. Though the words didn't make sense, her heart had jumped in recognition.

Since then, there had been many similar meetings with her body left behind. After those meetings, when all of a sudden she was back in her body, still busy preparing a meal or sweeping the floor, shining words lingered, words like the fragments of a mirror sending back the light.

'This fragrance drifting towards us, its source is none other than the tent of God's secrets.'

'It is the light of love which transforms the copper of your being into gold.'

From the shadows stretching outside in the courtyard, she could tell that hours had passed of which she knew nothing, except for

دوست

those words and a certain flavour she couldn't define. How is it that I am sitting with them while my body remains somewhere else? But the question had ceased to puzzle her and today she only longed to be back in the small study with Shams and Maulana, though she knew that her very desire was an obstacle. For it to happen, she had to be free, like a feather carried by the wind. But when, like today, the loneliness was too much and her heart longed for nourishment, it was difficult not to want to be sitting again in the small study with Maulana and Shams.

The sound of the door on her right broke in on her thoughts. She looked up and saw Hatije, who seemed uncertain of her welcome. The last time they had met, several weeks earlier, they had found they had nothing to say to each other and Hatije had left saddened. We don't live quite in the same world, Kimya had thought at the time. There were now too many things in her life that belonged to no one but Shams and Maulana. She could never explain to Hatije that there was another way of travelling, or that a shared silence could be more intimate than any conversation or physical contact. To Hatije silence was simply an obstacle to be overcome as quickly as possible.

Yet today Kimya was glad to see her friend. 'Come in,' she said, making room for Hatije to sit with her beside the fountain.

Hatije's face lit up.

'It's so hot today,' Kimya said, dipping her hands once again into the water and splashing her face.

Hatije was staring at her with a curiosity mixed with perplexity. 'I wanted to ask you ...' She sounded hesitant. 'We are going to Meram, to my Aunt Safia's to pick the first grapes of the season.

دوست

'Would you like to come?' She was looking at Kimya with expectation. 'Nuran is also coming,' she added as an encouragement.

The thought of Meram with its gardens and vines, its water mill and its small brooks running downhill was tempting. Meram was like an oasis, a refuge against the heat. Kimya had been there a few times. She remembered a day, several years earlier: the horse trotting along the road shaded by plane trees, herself, still a child, sitting in the carriage between Maulana and his young disciple, Husam ud din, and Sultan Walad and Ala ud din facing them, laughing at some private joke. And all along the wind rushing in their ears. She recalled other days spent sitting on the bank of the brook, listening to Maulana while eating halwa and the small cakes Kerra always prepared for such occasions. Kimya could almost feel the breeze cooled by the water. She could almost hear Maulana reciting poetry, his voice covered at times by the sound of the water wheel.

She hesitated. What would Shams say if he didn't find her when he came back?

Her hesitation didn't escape Hatije, who wrinkled her nose in that funny way of hers which meant she was getting upset. 'It's not good to be alone all the time. You need to see people.'

Kimya laughed. Unwittingly Hatije had borrowed her mother's tone of voice, determined and slightly sententious.

'So you're coming!' Hatije said, her face lightening.

'No, no, I'm not. It's already late and I don't think I should.'

'Oh, Kimya!' Hatije cried. 'You never go out. Look, it will do you good, and it will be cooler in Meram. And anyhow, we'll be back before dark,' she added reassuringly.

دوست

'I don't know. It's tempting,' Kimya admitted.

'Then come.' Hatije was becoming impatient. 'The carriage is ready and I promise we won't come back late.'

Kimya shut her eyes, imagining the coolness of the air in Meram, her friends and their giggling together. 'We will be back before dark, won't we?' she asked, repressing a vague feeling of apprehension.

'We will. I promised, didn't I?'

'Well ...' She was still hesitating. 'I think I'll come. Just let me wash my face.' She bent over the fountain, cupped some water in her hands, splashed her face once again and then tucked a few wisps of wet hair under her scarf. Hatije was already at the door.

Her basket was overflowing with grapes. She put it down and wiped the perspiration from her forehead. The small vineyard was bathing in red-gold light. Down the hill, half hidden by a row of poplars, the water wheel was sparkling in the light. 'Look, Hatije, Nuran, the rainbow in the water wheel.' Her two friends raised their heads.

'I can't see it,' said Nuran. 'Oh, yes, just about.' There in the spokes of the wheel, a rainbow was dancing through the water.

A bunch of grapes lit by the sun caught Kimya's eye. The last one, she thought, then I must go. She cut the stem with the small knife Hatije's aunt had lent her and started to hum a song. It was a song from her childhood, half buried in the past.

'You look a lot better, Kimya, than when you came,' Hatije's aunt remarked approvingly. She was a tall, cheerful woman. 'You have some colour now,' she said, 'and you have found your voice again.'

دوست

She stood, feet apart, looking at Kimya with a smile. 'Birds can't sing when they are kept in the dark,' she added.

Kimya blushed. Was that how people saw her and her life with Shams? A bird imprisoned in a cage?

'There are different birds and different songs.' The voice was deep and raucous. Startled, the four women turned towards the entrance of the garden where the voice was coming from and where the tall figure of Shams stood, ominous in the curved archway in the wall. Ignoring Kimya's companions, he said, 'I have been looking for you.'

Hastily she pulled her scarf, which had slipped down on her shoulders, back on her head. She heard reproach in his voice. Down at her feet the small knife she had been holding a moment earlier was lying abandoned.

Shams had already turned away. A feeling of despair mixed with fear overwhelmed her. She hurried to follow him, forgetting her basket. As she turned back, she caught Nuran's eyes, dark with anger and frustration. There, she thought, stood the simple, pleasant life she used to know and like, with its profusion and its beauty, and here she was, following the man she had willingly accepted as a husband, the man who, in spite of what everyone imagined, was offering her her real heart's desire. Yet she couldn't help feeling torn apart. What is it that I am following? she wondered.

Sitting in the carriage, she could only see Shams's back above her, obscuring the sky which was now just a glow of tender pink slowly turning dark. He was sitting next to the driver, leaving her alone in the back seat. She let the night enfold her, wishing the journey back to Konya would never end. It was not long, however,

191

before the sound of the horse's hooves on paved stones told her they were entering the city. She caught sight of the huge wooden gates, then of the flickering lights in the houses, their doors desperately opened to a still elusive coolness. Soon the horse stopped.

They entered their lodgings without exchanging a word and Shams went straight to his room. She stood in the entrance feeling slightly nauseous, her heart heavy. Perhaps Shams needed something to eat. She busied herself for a while, finding some relief in the activity. Her hands were trembling when she knocked at his door with a bowl of soup and a piece of bread on a tray. Without waiting for an answer, she opened the door. He was sitting near the window, apparently lost in his thoughts, and ignored her when she placed the tray on a small table beside his bed. She expected his usual words of thanks, but as she closed the door, she heard nothing but the silence tingling in her ears like the sound of bells ringing in the distance. She was unable to eat. She went to her room and, kneeling down, abandoned herself to helpless crying.

'O God, what do you want from me? I am married, yet without a husband. I am still a girl, yet without friends.'

She bent down until her forehead touched the ground where she remained prostrated, lost in her tears. It seemed that hours had passed when she finally raised her head. There was a large shadow in the doorway. The shadow was carrying a candle. Her body began to tremble uncontrollably. Shams walked in and knelt beside her.

'Kimya,' he whispered, 'Kimya, look at me.'

His hand was resting gently on her shoulder. There was no trace of anger or reproach in his voice. Still frightened, though, she

دوست

slowly raised her eyes. There was just enough light in the room for them to see each other's face and what she saw was so unexpected that she could not hold back a cry. The tenderness, the devotion in his eyes was so immense, so hardly bearable that she felt herself breaking into sobs. It was as if a dam had burst open. All the pain, the longing, the loneliness accumulated through the months rushed through her in a violent torrent. Shams put his arm around her and let her cry for a while.

'There, there, little one, there is nothing to fear.' She was holding tightly to him as if afraid to lose what she had just found.

'Love has no end. It is an ocean without shores,' he said. 'You have to learn to bear it.'

She looked at him again and as their eyes met a great wind seemed to fill the room, sweeping away the last traces of fear, of doubt, of anxiety. Hungrily their hands, their lips, searched for each other and found each other. Was it wind or fire that was engulfing them?

'Don't,' she heard him say, 'don't try to understand.'

Wave after wave came crashing, bringing them closer, then holding them apart as if suspended, then reuniting them. The great rhythm of life, the pulse of the earth and of the oceans was breaking through them, making them one with the One. In a whisper he said, 'The gift, the gift! Body knows the soul, soul the body.'

Yes, what a gift, she thought, astonished at her discovery. Man and woman, whole. A joy, a completeness was flooding her whole body. 'For ever and ever,' she heard herself say, and his voice far away, yet so close, like an echo, repeated, 'For ever and ever, in all eternity.'

دوست

They were lying in each other's arms, Kimya's head resting in the hollow of his shoulder.

'This, too, is prayer,' he said quietly.

A wave of gratitude overtook her, making her raise her head and stroke her cheek against the back of his hand. She felt herself drifting into memories. A stream rushing down the slope of the mountain, a golden sun sinking behind the mountain ridge, her mother's voice echoing in the distance, the face of Father Chrisostom curiously merging into Maulana's face.

'It's time to rest now,' she heard Shams whisper. She opened her eyes. He was standing above her, the candle in his hand. She caught a passing sadness in his eyes.

'There is so little time left,' he murmured, 'so little time ...'

What does he mean? she wondered. But he had already turned away and all she could see was his shadow outlined against the dim light in the background. Then the shadow disappeared. For a while she lay filled with a new happiness she had never imagined possible and slowly she drifted into sleep.

An angel was cradling her in his wings and she nestled in his light. 'You have very little time left, very little time,' the angel said matter-of-factly.

She woke up shaken, the words still resounding in her ears, the very same words Shams had spoken only a few hours earlier. The call to prayer caught her shivering in the morning coolness. In the prelude to dawn the birds had started their chatter. 'Oh, God,' she sighed, 'why is it that my heart is aching so much, with joy and pain more and more intertwined? What is happening to me?'

194

# – XXIV –

SINCE WHAT SHE CALLED 'HER WEDDING NIGHT', LIFE HAD acquired a new flavour. On the outside nothing had changed; she still went to the market with Kerra almost every morning, she still busied herself with the various tasks of housekeeping and she still spent long hours on her own when she prayed, read poetry or simply sat doing nothing. But the feeling of loneliness was gone. It was as if all those moments through the years when, for a while, the world around her lost its grip and her whole being was suffused with the deepest happiness had now merged into endless joy. A light was guiding her in each of her tasks, and that light was Shams's presence, now always with her, whether he was with her or not.

'Your heart is singing,' Kerra said to her one morning. 'I can almost hear it.'

Kimya blushed. It was true. Her heart was singing, though it was also aching, but of that she said nothing. 'My heart is too small,' she murmured, putting down the basket filled with fruit and vegetables she was carrying. 'It feels as if it wants to breathe and doesn't know how.'

'Your heart will find the way,' Kerra said matter-of-factly. She too had dropped her basket and they were facing each other. Kerra's eyes had taken on a sudden gravity. 'Our hearts have no limits,' she said. 'This aching is your heart expanding.'

دوست

As always, Kerra didn't need to be told, nor did she expect an answer to her remark. They picked up their baskets and walked home in silence.

It was late afternoon when Shams came home that day. He went straight to his room and left the door open. Kimya quickly prepared some tea. When she entered the room she found him, as she did so often, with eyes closed, lips moving silently. He looked like a rock or a mountain, impregnable.

'Stay,' he said, half opening his eyes for a second. From the tone of his voice she could tell this was not an order but an invitation, or perhaps a request. She sat down, her back against the wall. He started to recite the names of God. She too closed her eyes, letting the sacred sounds vibrate through her whole being. When she opened her eyes again it was dark and Shams was standing above her, a candle in his hand.

'This is one way of touching the boundaries of heaven,' he said, extending his hand to help her rise up, 'but one is not allowed to remain there, or at least not yet.' His voice was so low that it seemed that it was his shadow on the wall that was talking.

That night he came to her room and this time it was not a storm, but a gentle breeze that took hold of them. Slowly he undressed her and she lay there, feeling herself sinking into the same nothingness that she had encountered since she was a child on so many other occasions. But this time she was entering the nothingness in all consciousness, all the cells of her body drinking in a knowledge that was beyond words. They were touching each other, almost in awe, aware of something infinitely precious, infinitely fragile, now unfold-

196

ing. The tips of her fingers had become antennae, exploring a whole new way of tapping reality, her body leading her into a discovery that kept unfolding until, all of a sudden, she knew precisely what was happening: 'I'm disappearing into Being.' This was not a thought, rather knowledge branded on her mind. She uttered a cry, then everything vanished. When she regained consciousness, Shams was caressing her cheek. His eyes reflected the light of the candle burning beside them.

'God's ways of making Himself known are infinite,' he murmured dreamily.

A wave of gratitude swelled in her chest, bringing tears to her eyes.

'There is only Him,' he continued, 'the love you feel is Him.' He was talking firmly as if warning her. 'I am only His servant. You must never forget this.'

A wind of panic swept through her. Was he saying that she loved him too much, that her love for him was in some way blasphemous?

'You must be careful, little one,' he said, his voice full of tenderness. 'You must be careful not to confuse your love for me with your love for God.'

His hand was pressing her shoulder and she started to cry. How could he be so cruel? How was he able, always, to touch the very core of her being? She had given herself to him totally. Her body and her soul belonged to him, yet he had just made her aware that, truly, she couldn't tell whom she loved so overwhelmingly.

He was gently stroking away the tears running down her face, letting her absorb his words. She was at a loss. Whenever she reached a place where, at last, she thought she was secure, he immediately took it away from her, leaving her in total confusion once again. I don't even know what love is, she thought. This unbearable tangle of pain and joy, was this love? And was this what love did, to strip you of everything but your aching heart? She fell asleep as one escapes from a house on fire.

When she woke up Shams was gone, and from the light filtering through the narrow window she could tell she had missed the first prayer of the day. She stretched, then got up and started to dress. She would wear her dark red kaftan today, the one that made her eyes look even darker. So Hatije had once told her. She laughed at herself. What she wanted was to catch in Shams's eyes the same look of admiration she had caught on the day of their wedding. A sudden stabbing pain in her chest reminded her of Shams's warning not to forget God because of her love for him. But surely God, too, would be pleased if she looked pretty. So you want to be pretty, but pretty for whom? The question was irritating. She brushed it off, refusing to let it tarnish her present lightness of heart, and it was with some defiance that she put on the red kaftan.

Later on while sweeping the courtyard, she let her mind wander into remembering the sweetness of her night with Shams. It had been more than sweetness, she thought. She had understood something important, something that was now eluding her. What was it? She stopped sweeping. It had been like lightning, a sudden understanding. But what was it? It had expressed itself in words and it had to do with disappearing. Now it came back: 'I'm disappearing into

دوست

Being,' that was it. She closed her eyes, trying to catch the truth, the knowledge the words had carried. But the bright certitude that had flooded her then was now no more than a fleeting flavour, like the aftertaste of a dream already vanished. She sat down on the stone bench. Why couldn't she bring that knowledge back? Then from the depth of her being a voice surged. 'Stop struggling!' There was no doubt: this was Maulana urging her, and yet she was still sitting alone on the stone bench in the courtyard and in front of her, barred by a ray of sun, the door to the main house was shut. On the right, the cherry tree was gently rustling its leaves, agreeing that there was no reason to struggle for anything. 'Stop struggling.' The words imprinted themselves in her mind with unshakeable authority. Of course! That night, when the realisation had reached her, she was abandoned to the moment, receptive, in no way trying to grasp anything. That was the secret! She started to laugh. Here she had just caught another piece of knowledge, and like the previous one, it was already drifting away.

'God's knowledge is as free as a bird and so is your soul.' It was Maulana's voice again. She noticed a lark diving into the fountain. The bird hit the water, soared and disappeared as quickly as it had appeared. Looking at the water she wondered: The droplets shimmering in the light, were they aware that their spark came only from the sun and not from themselves?

It was several weeks since Shams had last visited her in her room. In the city the rumours and gossip were once more running rife. The thaw that had followed Shams's return had not lasted long, she thought. In spite of their promises to accept Shams and show him due respect, Maulana's students were already complaining. They had perhaps hoped that Shams, now endowed with a wife, would spend less time with their Master and that Maulana would start teaching them again. But their hopes had been dashed. Shams and Maulana were as inseparable as ever, and Maulana had clearly no intention of resuming his formal teaching. In the market people were whispering behind her back.

'Poor girl,' she overheard a woman saying one day, 'she is allowed no friends, no outings.'

'Well, she will get ill, if it goes on like that,' replied another woman.

No doubt that Shams coming to fetch her in Meram had been amply magnified and distorted. She turned round, taking no notice of the man staring at her behind his piles of vegetables. The two peasant women standing in front of the next stall wore the traditional baggy trousers women wear in the villages. Their shoulders were wrapped in shawls of muted colours, and for a split second there, in front of her, stood her mother, chatting with one of her neighbours. The two women turned their heads towards her, and the vision vanished. They made no effort to conceal their curiosity. Angry, Kimya walked away. Would people never stop talking about things they knew nothing about?

Days, then weeks passed. The cherry tree looked tired and its leaves were covered with dust. In the morning, though, the cooler air carried a reminder that summer was soon to end, and at night now Kimya cuddled under a blanket. Shams had not visited her since that night full of sweetness and confusion when she had discovered that one could know something and yet not understand it. 'There is a knowledge the mind knows nothing of,' Shams had told her once. At the time she had wondered what he meant. But the experience of that night had been exactly that: she had been given knowledge her mind could not grasp. Now, however, it all seemed to have happened a long time ago, in happier times. These days Shams kept her at a distance. When he came home he just nodded, looking stern, almost estranged. Was he angry with her for some unknown reason? One afternoon as she brought him a tray of food, he stopped her in her stride.

'You can leave it at the door, no need to come in.'

It was as if she had been stabbed. She retreated, fearing he would see the tears in her eyes. But he wouldn't of course. He didn't look at her any more. In fact he hardly spoke to her and when he did, it was only about trivial things, to remind her that the latch on the door needed oiling, or that she should ask Kerra for a few more candles. She searched for a reason for his behaviour. Was it because he had no love for her after all and had only been pretending? This she couldn't believe. Or was it because, as he had warned her, she risked forgetting God? The question kept gnawing at her. To have tasted of a love so complete, so totally fulfilling, and then to have lost it was like living with a knife planted in her heart. Never had she imagined one could feel so much pain. Her own sense of being was crumbling. She looked at herself and was surprised to find she still inhabited her body. So this is me, she thought, incredulous, for there was no I she could identify with any more. She remembered that in times of pain she used to find succour in prayer, but now she found herself unable to pray. All she could do was to

دوست

go through the days, attentive to her tasks, but cold inside, empty and numb. Buried in her were those precious moments when Shams had shared with her a thought, an idea, a memory. More than their physical intimacy, those moments had been the food her heart had fed on. Now those moments were no more, and her heart was left barren.

'You look very pale,' Kerra remarked one day. 'You're not taking good care of yourself.' She looked concerned, and Kimya sensed reproach in her voice. They were sitting together in the large kitchen busy shelling peas. They had been silent until then, both immersed in their task. There was something soothing in the calm rhythm of their activity: pressing the peas out of their pods with the thumb and letting them fall into the large clay bowl in front of them, then throwing the pods into a basket at their feet. It required just enough attention for the mind to remain steady while not demanding any thinking. Kerra had stopped, her hands resting on her lap.

'There are times,' she said, as if talking to herself, 'when the driest prayer is most pleasing to God. Then He, in His mercy, makes you aware how much you are missing Him.' She had taken Kimya's hand in hers and her eyes were full of tender care.

Kimya felt her throat tighten, and burst into tears. 'I can't pray,' she cried. 'My heart hurts too much.' It was a relief, at last, to confide in Kerra. She shook her head helplessly. 'I don't know how to stop the pain,' she murmured, tears streaming down her face.

'You can't stop it,' Kerra said firmly. 'When there is great pain, there are only three rules: not to push the pain away, not to try to understand it, and not to indulge in it.' Kerra's voice had a comfort-

دوست

ing certainty. 'Make yourself as open as a young tree caught in a storm. Let the storm bend you at its will, do not resist it, do not argue with it either – how could one argue with the wind and the rain? – and never, ever feel sorry for yourself.'

That night Kimya let the candle burn in her room. 'God, do not abandon me,' she cried out. But there was no one to answer her plea; she was crying into emptiness. She remembered Maulana's voice telling her not to struggle. Kerra's advice had been the same. And indeed, what else could she do but submit? Shams's ways were beyond understanding, and the pain tearing at her was too over-whelming to be fought. A tree caught in a raging storm, yes, that's what she was. Trees let the elements pass through them. They do not complain. They endure. The image was so vivid that though she was sitting on her bed, she felt herself standing straight, roots tying her to the ground.

It was several days before she realised that somewhere at the core of the storm still raging, somewhere under the turmoil, there was a point of stillness where, most incredibly, a dark, silent joy was waiting. Whenever she managed to keep her mind steady, her pain acted as a magnet, gathering all the scattered parts of herself, and allowing her at last to reach somewhere beyond the present moment, where that silent joy was also infinite peace and infinite power. It was curious, though, because the pain was still there, throbbing and – this was difficult to admit – necessary. But she was holding on to a rock, and as long as she held on to it, she wouldn't be blown away even though the point of stillness was faint. Like a reflection in a lake, it was at the mercy of the slightest breath of wind.

دوست

'This rock is your centre.' It was not a voice this time, but a silent message written on her mind in bright letters. 'The point of stillness is the meeting place. You may lose sight of it, but it never leaves you.'

The candle had burned out. She turned towards the wall and fell into a heavy sleep.

# – XXV –

SHE WAS STANDING IN THE ENTRANCE WHEN HE CAME HOME that evening and had no time to flee to her room as she had done so often recently. She had not yet lit the oil lamp and the place was growing dark. He looked at her, a quick glance, which left her trembling. Was she mistaken? She thought she had caught a shadow of compassion in his eyes. But he had already lowered his gaze and as he passed her, all she could see was his usual stern expression. He entered his room and instead of closing the door behind him as he had done so often in the last few weeks, he left it wide open. She saw him falling on his knees then prostrating himself. She remained standing in the hall, the silence ringing in her ears. She must have drawn back. Against her the wall felt rough. Unable to move, she let herself slide down. For a moment it was as if she were sinking into a dark smoothness, while at the same time being swept away. All she could do was close her eyes. She felt her heart pulsing irregularly, at times missing a beat. She had lost all sense of time when she became aware of his presence above her. Opening her eyes, she saw his tall figure slowly turning, turning, arms crossed over his chest, each hand resting on the opposite shoulder. His face was expressionless. She must have moved involuntarily. Half opening his eyes, he leaned towards her, took her hand and pulled her up.

205

دوست

'Let Him take over,' he murmured. 'Let Him take hold of your heart.'

At first she stumbled, then instinctively she copied him and crossed her arms over her chest, her feet guiding her into a slow spin. As she turned, she felt her heart stretching and the usual aching becoming sharper. But she would have willingly endured all the pain in the world for this. Eyes closed, she was spinning round a white flame, and this flame was her heart melting into an embrace that filled her with a joy hardly bearable.

'Enough!' His voice was soft. 'At first the heart can only take a sip at a time.'

She came back to herself reluctantly. Why couldn't he let her disappear, for ever cradled in that burning love? They were standing in the middle of the hall enfolded in darkness. The power around them was tangible. Under her hand, her heart throbbed like a wild animal trapped in a cage. They remained silent. She was trembling, and he put his hand on her shoulder to steady her.

'Losing oneself is the way,' he said. 'But it is not the goal. So great is His love that He wants you to know Him in all consciousness.'

Was he saying that she was not supposed to disappear? That she was not supposed to let herself melt completely, though it was her greatest desire?

'Go and rest,' he said. 'God has heard your prayer.'

She remembered that only the day before she had begged God not to abandon her and had thought He was not listening.

'God is always listening,' he said, catching her thought. She could not see his face, but there was a smile in his voice and for the first time in weeks, she could breathe freely again.

دوست

She woke up the next morning aware that the excruciating pain was gone, lifted. Nothing had changed, yet everything was as it should be. Her love for Shams, his ways with her, sometimes teacher, sometimes husband, sometimes – who knows? It was impossible to define. The feeling of gratitude was back and with it a sense of relief and wonder. She remembered the day she had witnessed Maulana spinning silently at the corner of a street. She had found the scene strange and slightly embarrassing. Later Maulana had said that most people were not ready to turn because they were not ready to be burned. At the time she had not understood what he meant by burning. Now she knew. To feel loved so completely, then to be suddenly abandoned had been worse than death. The burning had torn her apart.

She thought of the roses of Tabriz that Shams had once mentioned – long before their marriage – those same yellow roses with bloodstained hearts that someone had strewn in the entrance of their lodgings on the day of their wedding. 'These roses are close to God,' he had said, 'for only a bleeding heart can find Him.' His words had frightened her, but now she knew what he meant. She had felt abandoned by God as much as by Shams. In the midst of that total desolation, she had come to realise that instead of being anchored in God, she had become dependent on Shams's ever changing moods, and so lost her centre. Now she understood! Without centre there was only pain. That made the whole difference! Love, real love, was like looking at someone through God's window. The rest was attachment, and attachment was like falling out of the window. A feeling of relief flooded her. One could love someone without wanting anything from that person!

'Love is nothing but the breath of God breathing you out and breathing you in.'

She sat up, startled. Shams was standing in the doorway, staring at her. How long had he been there? It was embarrassing to be found still in bed, with the morning so advanced. But he didn't look reproachful. On the contrary, he seemed in a joyful mood.

'Doors are opening fast for you,' he remarked. 'You have no idea how blessed you are.'

She laughed. Was she blessed because he had just opened her door?

He shook his head, half amused, half taken aback by her laughter. 'You're right,' he said, turning away. 'I'm much too serious.' Then he was gone. She was still smiling to herself when she heard Hatije's voice.

'Kimya, are you there? I've brought you something you like.'

She had not seen Hatije since that day in Meram, more than two moons ago. It occurred to her that she had still been a child then. Now she was a woman. She put on her kaftan and went into the hall where Hatije was standing, a basket full of figs in her hands.

She took Hatije in her arms, feeling curiously maternal towards her. 'Hatije, it's good to see you,' she said.

They went to sit in the shade beside the fountain. Kimya brought a jug of fresh water and two goblets. The figs were as sweet as honey and the water was cool.

'We've been worrying about you,' Hatije was saying, 'but you look all right.' She sounded surprised. 'A bit thinner, though.'

Hatije was clearly expecting some comment, but Kimya had

دوست

nothing to say. Strange! The curiosity, the gossip, it all left her indifferent now. She looked at her friend, remembering the time when they couldn't stop chatting and laughing together. Their walks in Qamar al din Garden, their secret jokes – all this belonged to another time, another world she had somehow left behind. She could even tell when this had happened: it was that very day in Meram when Shams had come to fetch her. Unknowingly then, she had stepped into a more intense yet more peaceful world, freed from the turmoil that usually holds people.

'Kimya, I miss you,' Hatije said. 'It's so difficult to talk to you now. Why is that? What's the matter?' Her eyes were imploring.

'Nothing is the matter, but things have changed, Hatije. What I used to enjoy, I don't really care for any more.'

'Are you ill? Are you unhappy?' Hatije stared at her, looking worried.

'Happy?' The word was empty of meaning. There was only the real and the unreal. And what people called happiness and unhappiness, she thought, usually belonged to the unreal. Hatije was waiting.

'I'm not happy,' Kimya said, 'I'm' – she searched for the right words – 'I'm alive. I'm more alive than I have ever been. At times it hurts, but it's … it's glorious.' She closed her eyes for a moment. There were no words that could convey what she had so recently discovered. That each instant was an eternity, each breath a whole life: the weight of her hand on the edge of the fountain, the coolness of the wind on her skin, the rustling of leaves, everything was a gift offered freely for all to savour. 'If only we knew,' she murmured, half to herself, half to Hatije, whose eyes were wide with incomprehen-

209

sion and – it seemed – fear. Kimya forced a smile. There was no need to frighten Hatije.

'You must not worry, Hatije. Kerra had warned me that marrying Shams wouldn't be easy, and it's not, but you must believe me, Hatije, please, believe me, I couldn't ask for a greater gift.'

'Your eyes are so bright!' Hatije exclaimed. She was looking at Kimya with desperation. 'Why is it that I never understand you?'

'Hatije, it doesn't matter. We're different, that's all. All that matters is that everything is as He wishes, and it is, you know. It is.' She was quite vehement. 'How can I make you see that Shams is not some devil, that he is, on the contrary, God's envoy?'

Hatije looked contrite. 'Do you know that people are angrier with him than before he left?' she confessed. 'They say that he has bewitched Maulana and that he's driving you into despair.'

'Oh, Hatije, why do you have to listen to all that? I have heard this; Nuran already told me. But don't you know that none of it is true?'

Hatije blushed. So she half believed the gossips! Perhaps her visit was not as innocent as it seemed. She may have come to find out how Kimya was faring, but she also wanted to warn her about the mounting hostility towards Shams. They remained silent for a while, with only the sound of the fountain echoing around them.

'Shams could be in danger one day,' Hatije murmured. She was gazing at her hands, avoiding her friend's eyes.

Kimya's heart sank. Hatije was giving voice to a fear she had tried to dismiss, and yet …

'Shams is master of his destiny,' she heard herself say. The certainty from which her words had sprung surprised her. It did not

دوست

dispel the sinking feeling, though. Shams lived in the fire of the moment; he burned in it, but he also refused nothing of it. He embraced joy as well as pain, and no one would ever make him deviate from his path. His was a narrow one, like those paths carved into the edge of cliffs she had trodden in the village, each bend bringing a new challenge, a new danger, possibly death – but death was part of the bargain. Whenever death came, Shams would make it his own. She shivered. Why such dark thoughts?

'Nothing will happen to him unless he lets it happen,' she said. This was the truth, and it was as reassuring as it was frightening.

'Shams is as free as the wind, isn't he?' Hatije murmured, as though she understood.

Kimya nodded, relieved. They looked at each other and smiled at the same time. The sinking feeling had not completely gone, but Hatije was now holding her hand. It seemed that their friendship had passed the test, after all.

She took Hatije in her arms again and shut her eyes in silent thanks.

# – XXVI –

A FEW DAYS AFTER HATIJE'S VISIT KIMYA RAN INTO ALA UD DIN.
She was crossing the main courtyard on her way out when he
came in through the small door in the gate. He must have been riding
on the *maidan*. The curls of black hair on his forehead were wet with
perspiration.

'What else is there to do other than riding?' she had heard him
claim defiantly one day when Kerra remarked that he was hardly
ever at home. 'Father has no time for his students nor for his family
any more,' he had answered her sulkily.

'And you prefer the company of those who grumble about him
and about Shams,' Kerra had retorted. 'That way you can nurse your
unhappiness.' She was angry and so was he. They were interrupted
by Alim, who had just spilled his gruel on the floor and called
loudly for help. Taking advantage of the diversion, Ala ud din had
quickly left the room.

Now alone in the courtyard Kimya and Ala ud din were face to
face for the first time since the humiliating scolding he'd had from
Shams. For a second Ala ud din hesitated, then he walked on
without a word, his face closed in stubborn dismissal. She had time
enough, though, to catch the flash of angry sorrow in his eyes. He
looks like a wounded animal, she thought, ready to bite anyone
coming too close. The encounter left her with a bitter taste in her

mouth and her heart feeling heavy. I must not let Ala ud din and those like him disturb me. All is well, she reassured herself. In the end whatever happens is God's will. She had once heard Maulana say that men were no more than specks of dust rubbing against each other. 'Of course it is a little uncomfortable at times,' he had added with a laugh and it had made her laugh, too. Today the rubbing had certainly been uncomfortable, but that was not a reason to let herself be troubled by the sombre mood of Ala ud din.

Yet when she entered the narrow streets, Ala ud din's eyes full of pain and anger were still pursuing her. Lost in her thoughts, she had almost forgotten that she was on her way to deliver a small coat she had embroidered for a baby girl, the child of a cousin of Kerra who lived on the other side of the city. The shortest way was through the bazaar. She entered it, soon slowed down by the usual crowd thronging the narrow alleys. The air was thick with the smells of spices, smoke and sweat, and the cries of children mingled with the shouts of the stallholders and the women's sharp voices. Suddenly overwhelmed by it all and short of breath, she stopped near a vegetable stall. Her heart was aching more than usual. She noticed Hatije's mother standing a few steps away, engaged in intense conversation with another woman. Fortunately neither of them saw her, and Kimya quickly turned into a lane where she paused once again until her breathing eased and she could continue. She soon reached the quieter lanes of the jewellers, with their rows of neatly arranged bangles, brooches and earrings shimmering in the dimness. She could hear the ringing of the silversmiths hammering their wares not far away.

A light, clear beat caught her ear. Her heart jumped as though recognising the sound. It was like a voice singing above all the others, repeating a single note. It stopped, then started again, at times slowing down, at times ringing at a faster tempo. Hardly aware of what she was doing, she followed the sound. It led her to an alley of small dark shops, which looked more like caves than human dwellings. In front of each, a man was bent over an anvil, beating a piece of metal. She looked around but could not hear the clear beat any more, lost as it was in the clatter of all the silversmiths around her.

She walked a few more steps and entered another alley. This one seemed somehow familiar, and now the note was calling her again. I have been here before, but when? Her heart was trying to follow the rhythm of the hammer, stopping, starting again, slowing down, going faster. Her head began to spin. Her body felt so light that it seemed it might melt away. She leaned against the wall beside her. The man sitting at his anvil was turning a copper bowl of exquisite design on his knees and with a small, silver hammer beating out little dips and depressions in it. He raised his head and at that moment she recognised him. The man was Salah ud din Zarkob, Maulana's friend. She had once or twice taken a small gift or a message to him. This was why the place looked familiar. Salah ud din seemed surprised to see her.

'Oh, it's you, Kimya!' He smiled then frowned. 'Are you well?' He sounded concerned. 'Come and sit down. You are very pale.'

She obeyed as in a dream. Her heart was still throbbing irregularly. He indicated a small wooden stool somewhere in the darkness of his shop. All around, piles of bowls, trays, ewers and candlestick holders shone darkly in the light of an oil lamp, which deepened the

دوست

dimness rather than dissipated it.

She heard Salah ud din's voice saying, 'Let me offer you some tea.' He turned towards the street and called out, 'Ahmed, Ahmed, where are you?' A small boy appeared as if from nowhere. 'Bring us two glasses of tea, quick, this young lady needs comfort.'

'I don't know what happened to me,' Kimya said, embarrassed. 'I suddenly felt dizzy.'

Salah ud din looked at her with renewed attention. 'The heart is a strange guide,' he said, as if talking to himself. 'In the end this purveyor of life leads us towards our own annihilation.'

His words made her shiver. They carried a truth she vaguely recognised, and curiously, that truth felt like a frightening promise.

Ahmed was back with a brass tray bearing two steaming glasses of tea, which he carefully placed on a low table beside her, and then disappeared with the tray. They remained silent for a while, surrounded by the sound of the hammers, the two glasses of tea between them. The peace in the narrow space of the shop was soothing. She drank her tea in small, rapid sips. It tasted of lemon and orange blossom. Salah ud din stood next to her. He was of short stature, a compact, sturdy figure with large powerful hands.

'The hands of a silversmith,' he remarked, catching her staring at them. 'They shape and engrave metal. That's what they're good at.' He sighed as if seized by regret. 'This is easy work. There are other works, much greater ones that these hands can't perform.'

The passion burning in his eyes took her by surprise. She would never have suspected such fire in this usually quiet and self-effacing man.

'Have you heard of the philosopher's stone?' He seemed to be thinking aloud rather than talking to her. 'It's not really a stone – but do you know what it does?' He had lowered his voice, as if afraid that someone would hear the secret he was about to divulge. 'It transmutes copper into gold. That's what it does.' There was awe as well as passion in his voice. The flame of the oil lamp vacillated, sending ripples of light on to the piles of wares around them. He pulled another stool from the dark and sat down heavily, looking at her with searching eyes.

'I've often wondered.' He hesitated. 'I've often wondered how the copper feels while turning into gold. Does it feel frightened, joyful?' Again he seemed to hesitate. 'Perhaps … you can tell me.'

She drew back, unable to bear his intensity, only to be stopped by the wall against her back. Her movement had not escaped him and he stood up brusquely.

'Forgive me, Kimya Khatun, I have no right to ask. Please, forgive me. I'm an old fool.'

He had never addressed her in this formal way before. He suddenly looked frail and vulnerable, and she felt sorry for him.

'There's nothing to forgive,' she said, but she too had stood up.

They looked at each other, embarrassed.

'I'll ask Ahmed to accompany you back home.'

'No, no. I'll be all right.' She showed him the small parcel she was still holding in her hands and explained, 'I must deliver this to someone not far from here. I'll be all right,' she repeated.

'Are you sure?' Salah ud din did not seem convinced. 'You must take care of yourself.'

She nodded. 'I will. Thank you for the tea.'

Salah ud din nodded too. 'It was a pleasure,' he said, glad to

دوست

return to the safer mode of traditional politeness.

She walked a few steps and, turning for a second to look back, she saw him already bent over his anvil, the silver hammer in his hand. As she walked away, she noticed that, this time, the tempo of his hammer was slow and regular. She smiled to herself. What a craftsman of the heart you are, Salah ud din! She had never suspected it until this day. She sighed with a strange contentment and noticed that her heart had stopped aching. 'It knows how to breathe,' she told herself, surprised at her discovery. 'It has stretched.'

When a few minutes later she reached the house where she was to deliver her present, she wanted to sing, filled with gratitude.

'Oh, Kimya, it's so pretty!' the mother said, looking at the coat Kimya had embroidered. 'And it looks as if it will fit Malika just right. She's asleep at the moment,' she explained. 'I won't wake her up.'

She took a few small cakes out of a box and placed them on a plate. 'And how are you? How is Kerra?' The woman stopped. She didn't know whether to ask about Maulana because that would mean asking about Shams, and that was more than she could do. 'Would you like some tea?' she asked instead, pouring hot water into a jug.

Kimya accepted. 'Yes, everybody is in good health,' she said. 'And what about your husband?' She knew the man was a carpenter.

'Oh, he has more work than he needs,' the woman replied.

'These are busy times,' Kimya remarked. 'Konya is expanding.' The two women chatted for a while.

When Kimya left the sky was softening into a rose-tinted gold, as tender as God's whisper. This time she avoided the bazaar and took the longer way home, beside Qamar al din Garden.

The house was quiet when she entered it, except for a few sounds coming from the kitchen. She went straight to her room and lay on her bed, eyes closed, aware of the darkness rapidly spreading over the city and its inhabitants. The birds had stopped their evening chatter and in the distance a woman was calling, 'Fahik, are you coming?' In answer a dog started to bark.

She let the memories of the afternoon come back to her: the pain and the anger in Ala ud din's eyes, Salah ud din and his curious question, 'Have you heard of the philosopher's stone?' She could see the words dancing in front of her above the piles of wares glinting in the dark.

'Don't you know?' Maulana's presence filled the room and – there was no doubt – this was his voice, though she knew that if she opened her eyes no one would be there with her.

'The philosopher's stone is nothing but the purest part of you,' Maulana's voice was saying, and then he added, 'The work is almost done.'

She felt her heart jolting as if it had just received the answer to a question long held, a question she herself didn't know anything about. She had always thought that this philosopher's stone, wherever it was, had to do with the transformation of metals, as Salah ud din had confirmed. But Maulana was implying something else. She sighed. What had all that to do with her? And what was it that her heart knew that she didn't?

On the other side of the wall she could hear Alim moaning.

218

She stretched, to free herself out of her tiredness. It was time to go and help Kerra.

As the days passed the memory of the afternoon with Salah ud din lingered like a fragrance that kept floating around her, yet impossible to grasp. She could still hear Salah ud din and Maulana murmuring things about the philosopher's stone she didn't understand. She remembered her heart jolting from joy at Maulana's words, without being able to bring them back to her mind. This was not the first time her heart had run in front of her, hearing things she knew nothing of. For a few days the pain in her chest had eased, but today the pain had returned, more acute than ever, and she had noticed that she was getting more and more tired.

'You look very thin,' Kerra said one afternoon as they were sitting together in the kitchen. 'And you are so pale.'

Kimya remained silent, not knowing what to say.

'Are you eating enough?' Kerra asked, then she shook her head as if to say, 'Don't listen to me, I know my question is absurd.' Kerra, always so composed, was gazing at her hands, suddenly looking shy. Kimya had never seen her like that.

'You mustn't worry about me!' she exclaimed.

Kerra looked up. 'I know I shouldn't worry for you. What is happening to you is God's will, but ...' She didn't finish her sentence. Instead she pressed Kimya's hand and brusquely stood up. 'I am the one who told you it wouldn't be easy, and now look at me.' She smiled, a brave, almost apologetic, smile. ' Now I want you to escape.' She was angry with herself.

Again, Kimya didn't know what to say.

# – XXVII –

KIMYA STOOD IN THE KITCHEN, THINKING OF HER RECENT conversation with Kerra. A few weeks had gone by and her health had not been mentioned again. She looked outside. It was one of those grey November afternoons when the clouds feel like a weight on one's shoulder and the sky seems so close one could almost touch it. She had just emptied the water into a bowl from a large copper jug, so that it was ready to be filled again the next morning. There was not much more to do for the moment. Kerra had left some time earlier to visit a woman whose husband had recently died. Alim was asleep in a corner of the room, his head resting on a cushion, and the whole house was suspended in silence as if deserted, though, as usual, Maulana and Shams were shut away together in the study. The day seemed endless and she was feeling curiously tired. Perhaps she should rest for a while. The coloured cushions in the recess of the window were inviting. She sat down and shut her eyes. Her ears were ringing and she found it difficult to breathe. An invisible hand was squeezing her heart and with each breath a force, like the current in a stream swollen by the rain, was drawing her deeper into some unfathomable pit. Yet there was a strange joy at letting oneself be dragged away.

The first thing she saw when she opened her eyes was Kerra looking at her with concern. She realised she was lying in bed. She caught the sound of whispers somewhere behind Kerra. 'How is she? What happened?' That was Maulana's voice.

She, too, wondered what had happened. She looked at Kerra. 'Why am I in bed?'

'Sultan Walad found you in the kitchen just as I was coming back. You were unconscious. We carried you to your room. But, shush, you must not speak. You must rest.'

'I feel so weak,' Kimya murmured. All she wanted was to sleep. Even to keep her eyes open was an effort. She felt Kerra's hand on her arm.

'Drink this, it will make you feel better.'

Kerra pressed a goblet to her lips. The liquid tasted bitter. She swallowed it and fell asleep.

When she opened her eyes, she was alone. Somewhere in the house Alim was yelling at the top of his voice and, closer to her, just behind the wall, she could hear the clattering of pots and pans. There was something comforting in those sounds. Life was there, undisturbed, running its course. Yet she felt strangely unconcerned. She felt thirsty and, noticing the goblet on the stool beside her, she tried to reach it but it was just too far away; she couldn't raise her hand high enough and let it drop back on the blanket. She had never felt so weak. A thought crossed her mind. How long have I been here? At that moment, Kerra came in.

'You are awake, at last. I thought you would never open your eyes again.' She said that with a smile, as if joking, but she couldn't quite conceal the worry in her voice. 'How are you feeling today?'

221

دوست

she enquired.

'I'm all right, just a little weak, and' – Kimya paused; she was out of breath – 'I'm also quite thirsty.'

'Of course! Here is some water.' Kerra helped her raise her head and pressed the goblet to her lips.

She drank slowly, sip by sip. The water felt cool and refreshing. 'How long have I been ill?' she asked.

'Almost two weeks,' Kerra said. 'A doctor came. He said it was your heart and that you need to have a lot of rest.'

Two weeks! She remembered hardly anything at all of those days: Kerra's presence, some soup passing her lips, the flame of a candle wavering in the dark, and once, Shams's voice saying that God's will was to be listened to, not questioned, and, yes, that moment when a wave of tenderness had flooded her. She now recalled the words that had come to her then: 'I am nothing but this tenderness.' The feeling was still with her but fainter. She had let her head drop back against the cushions and now she wondered: Could it be that to love and to be loved were the same after all? She let the question drift away. All she wanted was peace. Near her was a soft rustling of leaves, or were they wings? Who was whispering to her ear? 'There comes a time when peace and life are like two rivers rushing together towards the same ocean.' She shut her eyes and fell asleep again.

She was standing in a place of undisturbed silence. Strange! It felt almost like indifference to the world, yet she had never felt so much love for all the people struggling in it. And it was as if she were six years old again and her friends were pulling at her kaftan, complaining that she was not paying attention to their games. She could hear Evdokia, her mother of long ago. 'This child worries me. What will become of her?'

'Look, Mama, I'm well. I am going where I always wanted to go. And I'm bringing you my joy, the joy that is in the mountain air, in the springs, in the murmur of the trees in the wind, in the radiance of dawn.' Now she was running down the stony path that led to the old crumbling house. She could see Farokh sitting on the stone bench next to the front door. She noticed that his hair had grown white and his face was furrowed. He was looking at her with astonishment, unable to speak, tears running down his cheeks. 'Baba!' she cried. The light around him and around the house was so intense that she shut her eyes, her lips suddenly dry. A voice reached her from afar: 'Drink a little, it will make you feel better.' Drops of water on her lips, the refreshing coolness of a mountain spring. She opened her eyes and saw Kerra's face leaning over her.

'Where am I? Where is Baba?'

'You are here in your room. You have not been very well lately.' Kerra's face looked strained. Her voice was hoarse.

'I'm well,' she reassured her in the same way she had tried to reassure her mother a moment earlier. 'Don't you see? I am going where I always wanted to go.' She noticed the tears welling up in Kerra's eyes, then a muffled noise behind her. Shams was standing beside the door, his face stern as always. But this time she could see through that severe look of his. He is like someone holding on for dear life in the midst of a storm, she thought, unflinching, yet utterly vulnerable. She shut her eyes again, filled by her love for him.

She was now standing in the middle of a field of lighted candles stretching as far as the horizon. The candles were of all sizes; some thin and long, some short and thick, their flames flickering as if moved by a breeze. 'The candles are all different,' the breeze whispered in her ear, 'but the flame is the same.' Yes, she thought, one vast brazier breathing in unison, and she was part of it, her chest rising and falling as the flames rose, then dropped, then rose again. She was now listening intently. The flames were turning into musical notes, crystal-like. They were springing from some inexhaustible fountain and were trying to tell her something. Slowly the notes became a murmur: 'The work is almost done.' Joy engulfed her. I have accomplished nothing, she thought, and the thought was as fresh and cool as the music she was hearing, yet my task is over. All of a sudden the flames leaped up, sending the music to a higher pitch, which turned the golden blaze into blinding radiance. 'You are each note and you are the music,' her heart was saying, but her heart was not hers any more, it was Shams's as well as Maulana's, Farokh's as well as Evdokia's. Her heart was the hearts of all those she had met and all those she didn't even know. She was drifting faster and faster. 'You are the candle, you are the flame, and you are the fire. You are the joy and the light. You are love. You are NO THING.' The tenderness in the words was the colour of the clouds in the autumn sky over Qamar al din Garden. 'This is only the beginning.'

The gratitude submerging her was hardly bearable. 'My heart is bursting open!' she cried. There was nothing but light flooding in.

224

# Epilogue

IT IS KNOWN THAT A WEEK AFTER KIMYA'S DEATH, SHAMS disappeared, this time for ever. There are many theories concerning this disappearance. The one that tends to prevail, probably because it is the most dramatic, is that he was murdered with the complicity of Ala ud din. There is no particular evidence to support this version, however. Sultan Walad, in his biographical poem about his father, makes no mention of Shams's murder; he seems in fact to dismiss the idea. Some chroniclers say that Shams returned to Tabriz, while one source mentions the city of Khuy as the place where Shams may have died on his journey to Tabriz. One thing only is certain: on a cold December night in Konya in 1248, Shams vanished and was never seen there again.

It is possible that Kimya's death was one of the factors that precipitated Shams's disappearance, but however devastated he may have been by her death, it is very unlikely that this was the main cause of it. What can perhaps be said is that Kimya's death was a marker, signalling the end of another relationship, that of Shams and Malauna; that is, Jalal ud din Rumi as he is better known in the West.

Kimya's transformation had taken place; her task in this world was finished. In a similar way, Rumi's transformation had also taken place, but his task was only beginning. In order for him to

دوست

accomplish that task, Shams had to leave, for his staying would have hampered Rumi. In both cases, Shams's work was over and destiny had to take its course.

*'... And the fire and the rose
are one.'*

T.S. ELIOT, *The Four Quartets*

# Glossary

*dervish*    someone who follows the Sufi way.

*doost*    دوست  the friend – the one I love.

*Khatun*    polite term for women, placed after the name.

*madrassa*    college, place of learning or school.

*maidan*    green outside the ramparts where parades took place and the young men rode and played polo.

*ney*    the reed flute played by Rumi at the beginning of his main work, the Masnavi.

*qadi*    a judge in Islamic law.

*Qalandar*    wandering dervish acting in apparent contradiction to religious law or social standards.

*rebab*    musical string instrument.

*Rum*    the Anatolian peninsula recently conquered by the Muslims from the Eastern Roman Empire.

*tanbur*    a kind of drum.

# Timeline

| | |
|---|---|
| 1190 | Frederic Barberossa stops in Konya on his way to Palestine, crosses the Taurus Mountains and drowns in Cilicia. |
| 1204 | Fourth Crusade – Sack of Constantinople by the Crusaders. |
| 1207 | Birth of Jalal ud din Rumi in Balkh province. |
| 1225 | Rumi marries Gohar Khatun, who bears him two sons: Sultan Walad and Ala ud din. (After her death Rumi marries Kerra Khatun, with whom he has a son and a daughter, Alim and Malika.) |
| 1229 | Rumi's family settles in Konya, Anatolia. |
| 1243 | The Seljuk army is defeated by the Mongols at Köse Dagh, a defeat which marks the end of the power of the Seljuks over Anatolia. |
| 1244 | Shams arrives in Konya. |
| 1246 | Shams's first disappearance. |
| 1248 | Shams's final disappearance. |

# About Kimya

Kimya did exist. She was part of Rumi's household and was married to Shams after his return from Damascus. A few chroniclers mention the marriage as an unhappy one.

# Acknowledgements

I would like to thank all the friends who have helped this book to come to life: Joy Carlson for her unlimited patience in reading my many awkward first versions, Elizabeth West for her unshaken faith in the book, and Robbie Lamming for her gentle pushes and advice all along the seemingly endless months it took to write it. And thank you, too, to Christine Bachmann for her patient editing of my somewhat fragile grammar, and, of course, a huge thank you to Jane Wisner for the love, care and fun she brought to polishing the whole manuscript.